THE BLACKBIRD THREAT

A Tale of the Fight
for Freedom and Survival

Filed by:
MARK A SCANTLAND

CAUTION:
Controlled Access

DEDICATION

I dedicate this book to my wife Karen, my children Michael, Christina, and Bryan. My family past and present who have put on a uniform to serve and defend our great country. A special thanks to my social media friends for your never-ending support and the inspiration I needed to write this book. I am forever grateful.

CHAPTER 1

June 13 at 2:27 a.m.

THE FULL MOON danced as it reflected off the waves of the Mediterranean Sea, fifteen miles off the coast of Syria, near the city of Jableh. Flying under the radar, two MH-60M Black Hawk helicopters were carrying twenty Navy SEALs. SEAL Team Six was on a mission to locate and recover a high-value target identified as Adnan Abadi. He was believed to have knowledge concerning a terrorist plot thought to occur soon in the United States.

"Lieutenant McCabe, sir, assets on the ground have verified LZ is clear of Syrian Forces. Command Center reports the mission is a go."

The two Black Hawk helicopters landed twelve miles north of Jableh and a half mile from the residence where Adnan Abadi was staying. The SEAL team silently moved through a vastly wooded orchard until they secured the area around the residence. It was an older two-story dark red brick home with many windows and two doorways, one front and one rear. Four soldiers guarded each side of the residence and surrounded the home.

Lieutenant McCabe and two other SEALs broke down the front entrance. With their night vision goggles and automatic weapons drawn they entered, crouching in attack position.

"Clear left," said one SEAL.

"Clear right," replied another as they advanced to

another room.

"Clear left, clear right, room clear," they whispered.

The lower level was now secure. Three more SEAL team members entered and started up the stairs in a staggered formation, with the first on the left side, the second four steps down on the right, and the third remained at the base of the stairs. The SEAL team member on the left side was at the top of the stairs when a dim light in the hallway came on. A lady appeared from the darkness and stood in front of them.

She immediately raised her hands over her head and asked, "Have you come for Adnan? I am his wife, Yana."

"Yes, where is he?" responded one of the SEALs in Arabic.

She pointed to a bedroom at the end of the hall.

"Sit down and stay down," the Navy SEAL told the woman as they began to clear the other rooms, finding two more women caregivers and a young girl.

They entered Adnan's darkly lit bedroom. It had a musky smell. There Adnan lay, in a hospital bed, attached to three IV bottles and an oxygen mask.

The first SEAL entered the bedroom and closed the pale blue window drapes.

"Adnan, Adnan."

Startled, he woke up to the SEAL's voice.

"We are here to take you to America, where you can receive the medical treatment you need. Your family can join you," said SEAL team leader Lieutenant Tony McCabe.

The elderly man smiled and only replied, "Allah is great."

With one SEAL member on each side of him, another drew a blood specimen for DNA confirmation.

"First, we have some questions to ask you before we can take you with us. Do you understand?"

Adnan nodded his head.

"Prove to us you are Adnan. Tell us what you know about Blackbird?" demanded the lieutenant.

"If I tell you, and they find out, they will murder me and my family. I don't worry about myself. I realize I'm dying of cancer. I just need my family protected," pleaded Adnan.

"Okay, we can protect your family. Tell us about Blackbird and we can be on our way. You will be admitted to the finest cancer treatment hospital in the world in less than forty-eight hours," Lieutenant McCabe assured him.

The woman being guarded by the chief petty officer leaned in. "He is late for his medication. I must give it to him now."

Nodding reluctantly, the SEAL team member moved aside. "Okay, hurry up."

The woman entered a bedroom and opened a drawer on the nightstand, then turned and showed the bottle of pills to the soldier guarding her. "Here they are."

"Lieutenant, sir, the woman says he is late for his meds." The soldier saw the desperation in her eyes. "Sir, permission to let her enter?"

"Okay, let her in."

"What about Blackbird?" Lieutenant McCabe asked Adnan again.

"Blackbird has been a long time in developing and will bring America to her knees soon."

Yana walked past the soldier at the door and turned toward Adnan. "You are late for your medicine, dear." She reached into her pocket, pulled out a bottle of white and blue capsules, and handed two of them to Adnan. She poured him a glass of water from a pitcher on the nightstand. He took a sip and handed the glass back to her.

Again, Lieutenant McCabe asked Adnan, "So, who is behind Blackbird, who is funding this?"

Yana took the pills and placed them back in her pocket as she leaned over Adnan and said, "I love you, Adnan, and I always will."

Suddenly, she had a small .380 pistol in her hand. She placed it beside his ear and pulled the trigger. The back of Adnan's head exploded, killing him instantly. She turned to point the pistol toward Lieutenant McCabe, who was standing on the other side of the bed. The SEAL team member on her side of the bed fired a short burst, center mass, into Yana.

She sank down and back with her head twisted, leaning against the nightstand next to the bed. Her color faded from her face. Her beautiful brown eyes stared vacantly as a large bloodstain spread across the front of her gown.

"Mission is now aborted; prepare to evacuate," Lieutenant McCabe ordered the other soldiers. "Secure all computers and cell phones and prepare to take the two other women and the girl back to the extraction point. They'll be safer with us."

The women, in a state of shock, offered no resistance. They immediately obeyed the soldiers' orders.

"How in the hell did this woman acquire a weapon, Chief Petty Officer?" the lieutenant asked.

"I don't know, sir. She was searched and contained with the others. The only time she was not with them was when she retrieved his medicine," replied the chief petty officer.

"We'll sort this out back at the base, now let's get the hell out of here," the lieutenant ordered.

Three minutes later all members met on the outside, just north of the residence. Suddenly small arms fire was directed toward them. Streaks of tracer bullets lit up the sky in random order.

THE BLACKBIRD THREAT

Lieutenant McCabe shouted, "Do not re-turn fire unless they pinpoint our exact location! We don't know if they are Syrian Rebels, Syrian Army, or Russians advisors. Move out! Go, go, go, move your asses!"

The team members, the two women, and the young girl, headed back into the woods toward the waiting Black Hawk helicopters.

Three SEAL team members stayed behind, protecting their rear. One by one they slowly moved back into the woods toward the others. The team arrived at the extraction point a few minutes later.

"All safe and accounted for, Lieutenant. Enemy forces on our six, two hundred meters and closing, sir. We still don't know who is firing at us," the chief reported.

"Get them saddled up, Chief. It's time to fly."

2:56 a.m.

The Black Hawks ascended into the moonlit sky as they received small arms fire. Both choppers returned fire.

"Captain, enemy ground radar has a lock on us!"

"Captain, missiles fired!" shouted the co-pilot.

"Brace for impact!" shouted the pilot over the intercom.

The Black Hawks went into evasive maneuvers as the two bright lights advanced toward them. The pilots deployed flares as a countermeasure against the missiles. The first missile followed the flare and missed, the second missile hit the Black Hawk as a giant fireball, lighting up the night sky. Hundreds of flaming, jagged pieces of the Black Hawk drifted downward into the black Sea.

Horrified by losing half the team, Lieutenant McCabe slammed his fist against the helicopter sidewall. He slid down into his seat with his hands on top of his helmet. He wiped a tear out of the corner of his eye, seeing his men seated in quiet agony. The young girl cried and rested her face on one woman's chest as the women comforted her. Shouting from the cockpit, the pilot gave command control the last location of the downed Black Hawk as a recovery team was dispatched to the scene. 'Operation Telescope' was a total failure.

CHAPTER 2

June 18 at 10:15 a.m.

INSIDE THE WHITE House Situation Room, Max Braude, director of the Counterterrorism Division of Homeland Security, was receiving a debriefing on the failed mission in Syria. In attendance were: Three-star Army General, Jamie Lee Martin, Joint Chiefs of Staff, Navy Admiral Riggs, Colonel Glass, Commander of Special Operations Command, the Secretary of State, the Director of the CIA, the President's Chief of Staff, and others from the State Department.

The Secretary of State said, "I must inform all of you the president is pissed with this predicament you put him in. I presume you have a viable cover story? The optics are terrible! Now I must go to Syria and Russia and explain to them we have no operations aimed at them."

Admiral Riggs spoke next. "The official story is that we lost a Black Hawk in a tragic routine nighttime training exercise over the Mediterranean."

The Secretary of State nodded his head in agreement.

General Jamie Martin spoke up. "Max, we obtained good intel from the two women retained from the mission. Our assumptions on Mr. Adnan and his wife were, in fact, correct. They were part of a terrorist network. They helped launder money for terrorist cells here in America. The NSA and FBI have analyzed the recovered hard drive; the results provided us with a list of e-mails and IP addresses to investigate."

"I believe the recovered cell phone is being analyzed as we speak," Max added. "With all the NSA data mining, we will have a long list of persons of interest. We will have our agents investigate them immediately."

"Max, the president has expressed concern about the vulnerability of our nuclear power plants. They are classified as hard targets for the terrorists. Is his concern valid?" General Martin asked.

Max began to explain, "As most of you know, there are sixty-one nuclear power plants, with a total of ninety-nine nuclear reactors, located in thirty states." He pointed toward the map on the wall. "All the nuclear plants have increased their security since 9/11. Security protocols have been revamped and tested. Advanced electronic security of the control systems has been installed, as well as all the physical perimeters being reviewed and updated.

Max stood and advanced on the map. He picked up the laser pointer. "Gentlemen, I must say that my deepest concerns are missiles being fired from freighters just off our coastlines. Once outside the twelve-mile limit, we have the burden of inadequate response time. As you have seen in the Iranian missile tests, some have employed mobile launchers that are easily installed on the deck of a freighter." Max waved the pointer at the coastlines. "With the thousands of miles of coastlines on the east and west coasts, then add the Gulf of Mexico and the Great Lakes, there is no target in America that a missile fired from a freighter couldn't strike. Put a nuclear warhead or EMP device on those missiles and millions will die.

"If our nuclear power plants come under an EMP attack..." Max paused speaking and looked everyone in the eye, giving time for the information to sink in.

"I was under the impression that steps have been taken to minimize the disaster," Colonel Glass said.

"They have, Colonel. However, if ninety percent are unaffected, we still could have nine reactors in meltdown. Casualties in the millions could be expected. Studies released in a 2004 congressional report on an EMP attack, resulting in the total destruction of our power grid, projected a ninety percent population reduction within the first year. The official estimated time was two to four years to rebuild the national power grid." Max returned to his chair. "FEMA has acquired food, medical, and other emergency supplies, but there is no way to take care of three hundred and twenty-five million Americans in case of such an event."

Max sat on the edge of his seat. He had been privy to this information for years and spent many a sleepless night because of it. "We feel our water supplies are soft targets. Shopping malls, schools, and municipalities are more probable targets. However, we cannot rule out any type of attack.

"That brings us to our latest intel." Max leaned back and took a deep breath. "We know there is a terrorist plot in progress called Blackbird. We don't know if this is an actual person, place, or codename, but it keeps surfacing more and more. The word Compton is of interest as well. We feel this might be a large-scale attack, based solely on the amount of chatter we have heard. We are in the process of forming an elite task force to investigate the top leads in the Blackbird threat. I will give you all a weekly report on their findings," Max concluded.

The Secretary of State nodded toward Max. "Thank you, Mr. Braude."

General Martin thanked Max as well.

"Are there any questions you want to ask Max, gentlemen?"

"What locations or countries have the communication intercepts originated from?" Marine General Josh Chambers asked.

"So far, General, twenty-three countries and counting. And as of today, you can add America and Belgium to the mix. Some of the scary phrases we have intercepted are: 'the end of America,' 'like the world has never seen,' 'death to Satan and world history will change forever.' Any way you look at it, none of this sounds good," Max stated with a sigh.

"No offense to you, Max, but why the hell are you running this operation instead of military intelligence?" asked Colonel Glass.

"None taken, Colonel. The main reason is if this Blackbird threat occurs on American soil, the president does not want the optics to appear to be a military takeover. The military will handle all overseas operations and backup as needed here in the States.

"I will use all the different departments together–FBI, ATF, Coast Guard, CIA, and the NSA–in an all-out effort. We are going to bend a few agency rules and try some new things," Max replied.

After a long pause, the president's chief of staff ended the meeting. "Thank you, gentlemen, this concludes the briefing. Good day."

CHAPTER 3

June 25 at 3:45 a.m.

JACK PUSHED BACK the sheets and hit the off button on the alarm clock. The day had finally arrived. First day back to work under a new top-secret pilot program with the Department of Homeland Security. It had been four long weeks since his previous assignment. He had no idea what to expect with this one, but was itching to get back to work.

Jack lay in bed, running a checklist through his head– *shower, finish packing, download and print boarding pass, drop off Sugar* (his miniature schnauzer) *at kid sister's house, and on to the airport.*

A sleepy Sugar tilted her head and looked at Jack as if expressing it was not the time to get up. Sugar knew this was not their usual routine.

Jack spoke to the dog. "You know the drill. Time to rise and shine and save the world."

Sugar crawled up the bed sheets and licked his nose as her stubby little tail wiggled wildly. She spun around and jumped off the bed, then looked back to see if he was coming.

Drying off after his shower, he gazed in the bathroom vanity mirror at his scars. Each one told a different story. Each scar was a chapter, and his story remained classified. Silent misery went along with the job when you were a secret agent. He laid out a three-piece dark blue suit, red tie, white shirt, and quickly shined his black wingtip shoes. Finally, he packed shorts, tee shirts, socks, and sneakers in his suitcase. Not knowing how long this assignment would last, he wondered, *Did I pack enough clothes?*

With everything ready and Sugar waiting by the front door, Jack armed the alarm system and grabbed Sugar's leash.

As he settled himself in his car, Jack called his sister, Liz. "Hey, Sis, I'm on my way. I'll be there in ten minutes. Do you want to drop me off at the airport, so you can keep my car? Or should I leave it at the airport? I'm running a little late."

"I'm up now, and I'll take you. Sugar can see you off," Liz replied.

"Perfect. Thanks, Sis." He felt fortunate to have such an awesome sister and best friend.

Liz sat at her kitchen table and took a sip of coffee. She wondered when Jack would retire. She knew not to ask questions he couldn't answer. She'd had an uneasy feeling about his work with the government ever since he told her he had a 'don't ask, don't tell' policy.

She was his Little Lizzie growing up, and Jack was all the family she had left. After her husband died, she left Texas and relocated back to her roots in Indiana. They were always close.

She adored Sugar as much as he did and was looking forward to taking care of her.

It was a warm, sunny day at the Indianapolis International Airport. A perfect day for flying. Looking out the large plate-glass window, he could see his plane taxi up to the gate.

He was thinking about all the times he had traveled to Washington, D.C. over the years and that maybe he was getting too old for this line of work. He never worried about himself, but he concentrated and worried about those he was working with and those he was trying to help.

He was hoping someone had a car waiting for him at the Washington airport or he might be late for his briefing. He called Max Braude and told him the flight was running a little late, and not to wait for him at the briefing.

After he finally boarded, he fell asleep, waking up just as the plane landed at the Dulles International Airport in Washington, D.C.

At the baggage claim area, Jack noticed a tall man in a dark suit and tie holding a sign with his name. *I guess Max wants me at the meeting on time.* Jack grabbed his luggage and smiled at the man holding the sign. "Hi, I'm Jack Jacobs."

"Follow me, sir."

Jack walked out to the curb and climbed into the back of a black limousine. "Man, the airport is hopping today. I picked a bad day to be late for my meeting. This limo doesn't have wings, does it?"

The driver smiled. "No worries, Mr. Jacobs." The driver flipped a switch. A loud siren and red and blue lights began flashing. "Buckle up, sir." The limousine kept increasing speed in heavy traffic as cars pulled over for them. The driver grinned in the rearview mirror. "I know all the shortcuts, Jack."

Jack returned his smile. "You know, I could get used to this, my friend."

* * *

Diane combed her long blonde hair. She took a long look in the mirror, finished putting on her makeup, and decided to remove her bright red lipstick. *I need to blend with the other women, not stand out. This is a work day, not an evening out. I hope Dad's advice about helping me move up the ladder at the NSA by volunteering for this assignment will pay off. He worked so hard pulling strings to get me this opportunity. I can't let him down.*

She picked up her phone. "Siri, call Daddy-o."

"Colonel Glass, how can I help you?"

"Hey, don't you have caller ID?"

The Colonel chuckled. "Yes, I do, my Princess Warrior, but I never take the time to see who is calling."

"I'm getting ready to head out to the briefing. I'll call you when I know more. I love you, Dad."

"I am proud of you, Diane. I know your mother would be too. Show them what you're made of, sweetheart. Love you too, bye."

With her suitcase in the car she began her journey, leaving Fort Meade behind her in the heavy traffic for the forty-five-minute drive to Washington, D.C.

"Siri, call Katia," Diane said.

"Hi, Diane, are you at your meeting?" asked Katia.

"I'm on my way there now. I was wondering if you could pick up my car and check on my apartment while I'm on this assignment? You can drive it all you want. I know it runs much better than your old Katmobile."

"Sure, no problem, sweetie."

"Okay, thanks so much. In my middle desk drawer at work, way in the back, is a key ring with an extra set of keys for the car and apartment. I'll let you know how the meeting goes. Wish me luck."

"You be careful, my best friend," Katia pleaded.

"I promise. Oh, and you be careful with my car. It has a lot of horses, four hundred thirty-five to be exact."

"Okay, I'll stay off the race track."

They both laughed because Katia loved Diane's white 2017 Mustang convertible.

It wouldn't be long until Diane found out what a field investigator did for Homeland Security, and just what kind of information the new secret program would entail. Now she would be stepping into the world she had been spying on for the last six years, and the thought sent shivers down her spine. *This is no time to be scared,* she told herself. *Any job that gets me away from sitting in front of that damn computer screen for eight to twelve hours a day can't be all bad.*

She was filled with excitement and looking forward to the new challenges, eager to prove women were just as good as any man at cyberwarfare. But she would miss being in the office with her friend Katia, and she would even miss her office manager, KJ Waters. She was aware this was probably just a temporary thing. She would still call Katia daily. *It's all good,* she told herself.

Fifty minutes later, Diane pulled into a parking garage beside the Homeland Security building. She informed the parking lot attendant her friend would be picking up her car later. She walked to the front of the massive building. Once inside the large lobby, she located the building's office directory. *There he is—Max Braude, director of Counterterrorism. Room 307.*

Once on the elevator, she couldn't help but think of the *Men in Black* movies. She smiled when she noticed the two men in dark suits and sunglasses accompanying her on her ride to the third floor. She didn't have any trouble locating room 307.

A middle-aged female receptionist was sitting behind a large oak desk. She smiled and asked, "Can I help you?"

"Yes, please. I'm Diane Glass. I have a meeting with Max

Braude."

"Max is next door in briefing room 309," the receptionist replied. "Nice to meet you, Diane. If you need anything just ask for me, Annie. There are donuts and coffee in the briefing room."

"Thank you, Annie. Nice to meet you, too. Have a nice day."

As she entered the briefing room, Max met her at the door. "Hi, Diane, nice to meet you." He extended his hand. "I've known your dad for many years. We are quite pleased to have you join us with this case." His handshake was firm and confident. "Your name tag is placed on the table at your assigned seat. Please help yourself to the pastries and coffee."

"Thanks. My dad has nothing but praise for you, Max. He says you are a man of great integrity and honor. I hope I never let either of you down." She smiled and headed for the coffee and donuts placed on a small table. It was a large pot of coffee sitting next to a stack of large red, white, and blue paper cups.

Even the cups are patriotic here.

She walked between the rows of tables and noted there were two chairs per table and three rows consisting of four tables, making a total of twelve tables. She did the math in her head. Twenty-four people would be working on this case. She found her seat at the last chair, at the last table, next to the wall. Sitting in the back of the room, Diane tried not to stare at the men as they came through the door.

Where are all the women? The seat beside her was still empty. She could see his name tag, Jack Jacobs. She counted twenty-two men now seated. A minute later a tall, handsome, dark-haired man with a tight, chiseled body walked through the door. *This must be Jack.* Max greeted him. *He can sit by me anytime.*

16

THE BLACKBIRD THREAT

To her disappointment, he sat down in the first row.

Max looked at his watch as he walked toward the door. "There you are. I was just about ready to give up on you," he said.

Jack was an older man with graying hair on his temples, thinning on top. *He is as old as my dad,* she thought, *but not in as good shape, and he slouches a little when he walks.*

He grabbed two donuts and a cup of coffee. Max pointed the way to his chair. He sat down, nearly spilling his coffee on his folder marked Top Secret. Diane wanted to laugh but knew better.

CHAPTER 4

Monday, June 25 at 09:15 a.m.
Washington, D.C.
Office of Homeland Security
Room 309

JACK KNEW HE was running late as he opened the door and his old friend Max was there to greet him. "Sorry, I got held up at the airport. Stupid TSA didn't believe who I was!" He picked up a couple of donuts and poured a cup of coffee.

"Your seat is over there, Jack." Max pointed.

Jack saw the only empty chair at the far table in the back of the room, right next to a beautiful young woman. He sat down beside her. *I wonder what she is doing here?*

"Good morning, lady and gentlemen. My name is Max Braude. I'm the director of operations of counterterrorism here at Homeland Security. You, twenty-four people, have been selected out of thousands of applicants. You are the best of the best! In this room, we have FBI, Special Operations SEAL Team Six, as well as Delta Force, CIA, ATF, ICE, and NSA personnel." Max smiled. He was proud of the team he had gathered. "The person sitting at your table is your partner for this assignment. Your life and the future of America may depend on you and your partner, so you must work together twenty-four hours a day, seven days a week. If, for any reason, you cannot or will not work together, you must notify me at once, and you both will be removed from the program.

THE BLACKBIRD THREAT

Unless you are Jesus H. Christ, saving the world is a team sport, and you are my team. We are here to serve and protect our great country and, by God, we will on my watch. Understood?"

Jack glanced around the room, and saw some familiar faces. He had either worked with them or crossed paths while working on other investigations. *Max must really be feeling the heat, he has all the big guns working this case, and I wonder where Miss America fits in?*

"As you know, some great work has taken place at the NSA with data mining, and we now have more persons of interest, regarding terrorist threats, than we can shake a stick at. With the three-hop searches of e-mails and now with social media, Homeland Security is flooded with suspects. As *we* cross this over with keyword usage and cell phone voiceprints, *we* can track their networks, see these terrorist cells evolve, and know what they are planning." He paused and took a deep breath. "Your job is to assist us with the tracking information and to check these people out. And, if you should find yourself in the middle of a terrorist's act, use all means and force necessary to stop it! No pressure here, but we cannot and will not fail! You have the full force of all the branches of government behind you!" Again, he paused and paced back and forth in front of the room. He wore an intense look on his face, making eye contact with each person in attendance.

"Today some of you are being paired up with someone from a different branch of government service. We think your different experiences combined will be a little more effective way to combat and halt potential terrorist attacks. We are thinking out of the box here with this approach. So, how you handle this will determine if this program expands or gets dropped."

"Okay, the packet in front of you is marked Eyes Only, Top-Secret. Inside, you will find the rules of conduct and rules of engagement with persons of interest, as well as your personal contact information, wills, life insurance, and notifications for next of kin. You will read, sign, and date. Do this now."

A short time later Max said, "Now, you all will be operating in a lone-wolf mode, meaning we are giving you enough trust and a rope to hang yourself! You will receive daily updates and targets, which are the people of interest. Oh, and I will need a daily progress report from each team. You will not know where the other teams are located or what their missions are unless I think it is necessary. This for your protection.

"After the briefing, you will be issued a government vehicle, a credit card, ID, and a cell phone. You must use this phone only to communicate with me. You will be issued a sidearm if you don't already have one. Oh, one other thing, keep all personal messages on your own cell phone, not on mine, and all government e-mails on government encrypted devices! No one here named Hillary here, right?" Max asked. "Are there any questions?"

Jack raised his hand.

"Go ahead, Jack."

"How will we handle our day-to-day travel and living expenses, Max?"

"Okay, each of you will be issued a standard government credit/debit card, and three hundred dollars per diem will be added daily to your account. If for some reason you need more, call me and we'll talk about it. After you leave here, you will go down to the first floor, to the Procurement and Supply office, and see Ms. Linell Gibson. She will see that you get all the gear you need. Any other questions? No? Great, I look forward to putting the hurt on these murdering sons of bitches with you. That is all for now.

"Take time to get to know your partner now, and standby for your orders no later than Wednesday. Each of you has a room reserved for you at the hotel down the street. Good luck. Dismissed."

Still seated, Jack turned to the young lady. "Hi, partner, my name is Mike Jacobs, but everyone calls me Jack." He stuck his hand out for her to shake, which she did.

"Diane Glass."

Jack smiled. "Well, you don't look like you fit in with this crowd. You're much too good-looking."

Diane smiled back. "That's funny, you all look the same to me."

Jack chuckled. "Well, I guess I had that one coming."

Still laughing together, they met Max standing at the door.

"Jack, I see you met your partner," Max said as he turned to Diane. "I talked to your dad, and the Colonel says I'd better take good care of you. I assured him we would, right, Jack?"

Jack was thinking he knew of a Colonel Glass in Iraq. A badass Army Ranger colonel nicknamed Bulletproof Glass. Jack looked at Diane and asked, "Is your dad Colonel Jim 'Bulletproof' Glass?"

"Yes, he is, or he was. He was once shot in the leg and it made everyone drop the nickname."

"Well, Max, I'd better take good care of Diane. The last thing I need is an Army Ranger colonel, and now a Delta Force commander, pissed off at me," Jack said.

Diane looked at Jack and nodded her head. "That's right." She gave him a wicked grin.

As he returned her smile, Jack was wondering if this was going to be a more stressful job, considering who Diane's father was. "Let's go downstairs and see what kind of toys the U.S. of A. has for us."

Max slapped Jack on the back. "Nothing but the best, Jack! I'll call you tomorrow and tell you where you're going. Talk to you soon."

A few minutes later, Jack and Diane were downstairs waiting to see a Ms. Linell Gibson about receiving their government-issued gear. After sitting in a waiting area for a while, Jack turned to Diane. "This is as bad as waiting at a doctor's office."

After a long pause Diane asked, "Well, Mike, why the hell does everyone call you Jack?"

"It's a long story."

"Apparently, I have the time for it."

Jack started to explain. "When I was in high school in Indiana my junior year, I was the quarterback on the football team, and we had the worst offensive line that year in the history of high school football. I would always have to run for my life while trying to throw a pass. One of the coaches kept saying I ran like a jackrabbit, which kind of stuck. Ironically, I also was dating a cheerleader named Diane. It was 1982 and John Mellencamp wrote a popular song that year named 'Jack and Diane,' so between football and the song I became 'Jack.' Even my parents started calling me Jack."

"So, how did it go with the cheerleader?"

"Well, we lost most of the games that year and she dumped me. She traded me in for a basketball player."

"That's some story and kind of sad."

"Not really. The last I heard, Diane had five kids and her husband was a used car salesman." Jack grinned.

Ms. Linell Gibson poked her head out of her office door. "Jack and Diane, please step into my office." She waved her hand toward some chairs. "Have a seat. This will only take a few minutes."

Linell's office was painted a pale, yellow color. On her desk was a pile of papers, a desktop computer, and a phone, as well as pictures of her and her children attending a rock concert. On the wall was a picture of the president, and the secretary of Homeland Security.

"Wow, I have been busy processing your equipment request, you guys hit the lottery." She laughed. "I don't remember anyone being issued this much for a field assignment." She reached into her desk drawer and pulled out two credit cards and Homeland Security ID badges. "I need you to sign here for the badges and here for the credit cards. Your vehicle is a new Chevy Suburban. Rumor has it this vehicle was headed for the Secret Service but was re-assigned to you at the last minute. You must have friends in high places?" She smiled. "Okay, in your Suburban you will have two laptops, two smartphones, two wireless transceivers—in short, a James Bond spy kit." She laughed. "AKA surveillance system. One Stingray interceptor cell tower kit, two HK MP7-1A submachine guns with five 20-round magazines each, and two Glock 22 Gen4 pistols with four 15-round, .40 Cal. magazines each.

"Diane, I can get you a smaller and lighter Glock 26 if you want," she offered.

"Thanks, Linell, but I prefer the twenty-two. I qualified expert with one."

"That's awesome." She reached inside her middle desk drawer and rubber stamped their paperwork. "Also, two bulletproof vests and two sets of handcuffs. We will have your Suburban loaded and ready to go by 7:00 a.m. That's it, all done. Any questions?"

Jack felt like he should raise his hand. "What is a Stingray interceptor? That's a new one for me."

Diane answered, "It mimics a cell phone tower, intercepts the call, and then sends it to a real cell tower and allows us to listen in. You can also triangulate, using other cell towers, and get a fixed position within a few feet of the location of the caller."

Ms. Gibson looked at Jack and turned to Diane. "Take good care of this equipment. The Stingray has all the newest upgrades and alone cost about as much as a small house." She gave them a stern look. "Wishing you both good luck. Stay safe."

Jack and Diane both thanked Linell.

A few minutes later, with suitcases in hand, they went strolling down the sidewalk to their hotel.

Jack yawned. "Well, it's about nap time for me."

Diane looked at Jack and shook her head. "I hope the hotel has a gym, because I need to work out."

After they received their hotel keys, Jack turned to Diane. "I'll call you in the morning. Have a great rest-of-your-day."

"You too, partner. Rest up, old man."

Jack ordered lunch from room service, unpacked his laptop, and quickly typed his new partner's name into the Google search bar and on a host of government websites. He found that Diane Glass was twenty-eight years old, daughter of Army Ranger Special Ops Commander Colonel Jim Glass, and a straight-A college student at Georgia Tech. She made the Dean's list, carrying a double major in Computer Science and Information Technology. She was a member of the track team, an alternate on the U.S. Women's Olympic Shooting Team, and her hobbies listed were swimming and karate with a rank of ninth-degree black belt. She had no history of working, which meant she was recruited by the NSA right out of college.

Yep, she's a daddy's girl. A real Princess Rambo.

Jack locked his fingers behind his head and leaned back in his chair, a big grin forming on his lips.

* * *

Diane unpacked her workout clothes and went downstairs to the gym. She ran five miles on the treadmill, hardly breaking a sweat, lifted some free weights, and practiced her karate kicks on a punching bag. Returning to her room she showered, ordered a salad for lunch, and called Katia.

"Hey, could you do me a big favor and look up any files on a Michael Jacobs of Indiana. He is my partner on this investigation. His nickname is Jack, and goes by Jack Jacobs; he's approximately fifty-something years old, and probably served in the military or CIA or some other federal agency."

"What's he like, is he handsome and a nice person?"

"He's not bad looking, seems nice and a bit of a goofball to me. He's not straight-laced like I thought he would be. He is very free with his advice and taking me under his wing. Which is kind of comforting and at the same time annoying? I get the feeling he might be afraid of my dad," she laughed. "So, if you get a minute, run him through our databases for me, okay?"

Katia said, "Sure, dear, I'll call you back soon, I hear the boss coming... got to go!"

"Thanks, K."

While Diane waited for Katia to call back, she watched her favorite cable news channel, WWN, Worldwide News. A story about a weather satellite, launched as a joint effort by Iran and North Korea, caught her attention.

Is this really a weather satellite or is it a spy satellite?

An hour later, Katia called. "Well, your partner is a bit of a mystery. I couldn't find out much other than surface data." Katia sighed. "I tried. Here's what I found out. He has a teaching degree and taught high school history for one year. He then joined the army, went to OCS, and became an officer. He was promoted to captain and spent the rest of his military service in army intelligence. However, most of his time in the army is classified, either inaccessible or eradicated. He left four years later and went to work with the CIA as a 'special skills operator,' and with Blackwater as a 'security consultant.' His current assignment is listed as contract investigator for Homeland Security. That's all I got, Diane.

"How did the meeting go? Are you happy to be involved with this investigation? Did you get a chance to meet the other women working on the case?"

"Well, it's a little early to say how it's going, and there aren't any other ladies on the case, just me. The guys are all Special Ops, CIA, and FBI, or some other federal law enforcement agency. I'll call you tomorrow when I have a better feel for what I'm going to do. Goodnight, my friend."

"Goodnight. Be careful, my friend," Katia replied.

Diane went to bed late that night, not having any idea what tomorrow would bring. She had many more questions than answers on what her role was or what they expected of her.

CHAPTER 5

June 26 at 9:00 a.m.
Homeland Security Headquarters
Room 309

MAX MET WITH Diane and Jack and briefed them about the mission in Syria. Diane knew about Blackbird and Compton as keywords of interest from when she worked at the NSA.

"The intel from Syria found recurring tweets, emails, and posts to Columbus, Ohio; Dearborn, Michigan; Irving, Texas; Los Angeles; and Wichita, Kansas. I'm assigning you two to Columbus first, and then on to Dearborn. You will proceed wherever the intelligence leads you," Max instructed.

"I haven't been to Columbus in a long time," Jack said over the rim of his mug. "It's a big college town, and the home of Ohio State University." He turned his attention to Diane. "There is a very large number of foreign exchange students."

"I'm young enough to fit in with that crowd," Diane suggested.

Max nodded. "You could pass for a freshman."

"My mom looked young for her age too." Diane beamed under his compliment.

Max leaned forward in his chair and pushed the plate of donuts toward Jack. "We have narrowed down your person of interest to a three-block location on West Fifth Street. You'll need to pinpoint the specific location further when you arrive on location."

Jack took another donut and refilled his cup of coffee. "Roger that."

A short time later, Jack and Diane changed into their travel clothes–shorts and tee shirts. Diane added a pair of oversized sunglasses and pulled her hair up into a ponytail. They loaded their suitcases into the shiny black Suburban and left Washington, D.C. behind.

Jack took the wheel first. "We need to make this black Suburban look like a family Suburban instead of a Secret Service vehicle."

Diane crawled into the passenger seat. "We can pick up some family decals to stick on the rear window. Maybe one of those with the man, woman, dog, and cat."

Jack smiled at her idea that someone might think they were a couple, or maybe she was thinking father and daughter. "Great idea, and maybe an NRA sticker or 'My Other Car is a Porsche.'"

"Maybe some beads for the rearview mirror too. We could get some cool seat covers. I vote for cats."

Jack put the SUV in gear. "I'm more into wolves."

Diane rolled her eyes at him and changed the subject. "We have some interesting things back there, don't you think?"

"What? The pistols and submachine guns, or our suitcases?" he replied with a smile.

"Oh, how do we explain our traveling together, Jack? Am I your young trophy wife with daddy issues or am I your brat daughter?"

Jack laughed. "Well, I'm not certain I am trophy-wife-worthy material, so I believe the daughter might be a bit more believable."

"Okay, daughter I am. I've had some experience with that."

Jack turned on the radio. "Is classic rock okay with you?"

"That's great. I'm an eighties rock girl."

"Well, that's a relief. I was afraid you were some kind of hardcore hip-hop-rap-thingy person, and that would just drive me nuts." He grinned, shaking his head.

After a few hours of driving on the interstate, Jack turned to Diane. "I wonder if our Suburban has armor plating and bulletproof glass? It seems like it drives and handles like a normal Suburban. Linell acted like this Suburban was pretty special, though?"

"I can tell you if it is plated or not."

"Really? How?"

"Give me a minute." Diane looked at her phone. "A Suburban with a V8 engine averages twenty-three miles per gallon. If this one gets that, then no, it's not armor plated. Due to the added weight, it should get less gas mileage."

Jack checked the Suburban's trip computer. "Awesome, we're averaging seventeen miles per gallon. First time in my life I'm happy to get poor gas mileage." They both chuckled.

"I need to call my dad and let him know I'm okay, or else he might send out some drones looking for me," she said, shaking her head. "Siri, call Daddy-o."

"Hi, Princess, I checked my caller ID this time."

Diane could almost hear the smile in her father's voice. "I just called to tell you I'm fine, and Jack and I are on our way to Columbus, Ohio to gather some intel on a person of interest."

"Who is Jack?"

"Jack Jacobs. He's my partner from Homeland Security, an ex-army officer and ex-CIA field agent."

"Is Jack with you now?"

"Yes, he's driving. We have a really awesome Suburban that was going to the Secret Service, but somehow we ended up with it." She stage whispered into the phone, "We think it's even armor-plated."

"I'm glad to hear Max is taking good care of you! Let me talk to Jack."

"Okay... here he is," Diane said as she handed Jack her phone.

Jack put the phone to his ear. "Good afternoon, Colonel Glass."

"Hi, Jack, I just wanted you to know that Diane means the world to me, and I appreciate you working with her."

"I'm sure Diane will take good care of me too, sir."

"Take good care of *you*? What the hell do you mean by that, Jacobs?!" the colonel asked. He had obviously misinterpreted Jack.

Jack hurried to recover his lost ground. "I-I meant to say, sir... it is an honor and a privilege to serve our great country with your daughter. Never have I seen someone with such intelligence and skills. Not only can she outrun me, and outshoot me, she can probably kick my ass, sir. You raised her the right way, the perfect daughter, Colonel... Sir!"

"Okay, carry on, Jack. Put Diane back on."

She spoke quietly, almost mumbling, to her dad for the next several minutes and ended by saying, "I love you, Dad. Bye for now."

Diane plugged her phone into the charger, then turned to Jack with a grin. "Sucking up to the colonel, Jack?"

"Was I that obvious?" Jack asked, laughing.

"Oh yeah, even your face turned red. But Dad kind of expects it, or should I say, sometimes he demands it."

THE BLACKBIRD THREAT

"How many Special Operators, Delta Force, Rangers, and Green Berets are under your dad's command… six thousand?"

"That's classified. I think you are outnumbered a little on this one," she teased.

Jack glanced at her with a serious look on his face. "I do want you to know that I have your back. I will die if necessary, to protect you and our country. In this business, we could be walking into a trap at any moment. We are the tip of the intelligence spear."

"I will do my best to protect you as well, partner. I'll leave the dying part to anyone who comes up against us."

"Well, with that being said, I'm starved. Let's find someplace to eat and then you can drive for a while if you want."

"Sounds good to me."

They stopped for lunch at a truck stop at the next exit off the interstate.

Diane eyed Jack over the rim of her coffee cup. "What did you do last night, besides Google me?"

"After studying your profile, I just watched a little TV." Jack took a bite of his pie, then pointed his fork at her. "Now then, Princess Rambo, where did you find any info on me? Most should still be classified."

"As you know, we girls have our ways." She smiled and took another sip of her coffee. "So, why did you stop teaching history after just one year?"

"None of my students cared about lessons from the past–not one. Their idea of history was what happened at the party last night or who was someone's ex-boyfriend or girlfriend." Jack put down his fork and wiped his lips with his napkin. "After being discouraged by teaching, I joined the army, went to OCS, became a captain, and was involved with military intelligence. After my tour was up, it wasn't long before I was recruited by the CIA. They wanted me to work in the Middle East with special intelligence operations. I also worked for Blackwater as a security specialist in Iraq and all over the Middle East."

He picked up his own mug and blew on the hot coffee for a moment before taking a sip. "Your turn."

Diane ran her thumb over the handle of her mug in thought. "Well, as you might guess, I was born in an army hospital. When I was ten, my mom died in a car crash coming home from the grocery store. A guy blew through a red light and T-boned her car. That was the lowest point of my life. I still see her in my dreams. It took years for me to accept the fact that she wasn't coming back. Who dies coming home from the store?

"Dad did the best he could." Diane realized she was fiddling with her mug and put it down. She picked up her fork and took a bit of her pie. "I was raised as a tomboy. My dad used to call me a real tough little cookie. He was always pushing me to be the best I could and to be the strongest mentally. Pretty soon it became a personal challenge. I wanted to be the best in everything I did. I felt if I didn't finish first, I failed him. Second place was unacceptable. It didn't matter whether it was in the classroom or in sports; I always had to be number one. I was his Princess Warrior." She finished up her pie. "Believe me, there is a reason why they don't put twelve-year-olds in army basic training. If I made him mad, he would sometimes get in my face and scream at me like a drill sergeant! I had no mother to run to, no space to hide. I knew he loved me very much, I just didn't understand his reasons."

"No time for boys growing up?" Jack asked, trying to

lighten up her mood.

"Sure, lots of them, but none of them lasted very long. If I didn't beat them up, they were afraid my dad would. It's kind of funny now, but not so much back then."

The waitress showed up at their table to offer more coffee. They both allowed her to top off their cups.

Diane thanked the waitress and then went on, once the woman left for the next table. "The gym was my real salvation. After I learned how to make and keep friends, I was happy there most of the time. My childhood was on army bases, wherever Dad was stationed. I was always in a gym or on a shooting range. You know, to quote Vince Lombardi, 'Perfect practice makes perfect.'"

"Great quote," Jack commented. "I knew a field operative who used it, and was exceptional with disguises."

"I bet he was an interesting guy to work with," Diane commented.

"Gal," Jack corrected. "You're not my first female partner." He cleared his throat. "Go on. I didn't mean to interrupt."

"Oh, well, not much more to tell. I graduated with honors in high school and received a scholarship to Georgia Tech, where I majored in Computer Science and Information Technology."

"So, no reading romance novels for you?" Jack kidded.

"Hardly; I liked to study military codes. Mostly World War Two stuff like the Germans, Japanese, and French Resistance used. I was a code nerd, so I was a natural with computers."

The waitress asked if they needed another fill-up on their coffee. They both declined.

"Not into sports?" Jack asked as he finished off his cup.

"On the contrary, I was a member of the track team. I ran with Dad, five miles every day, since the age of twelve. I ran the five thousand-meter races just to keep up my normal routine."

"And your karate skills I read about?"

The waitress started to put their check on the table, but Jack had his card out before she had a chance to put it down. He handed it to her and she went off to run it.

"I'm most proud of those skills," Diane confessed. "I received my 9th-degree black belt in karate around my junior year. I tried out for the women's Olympic shooting team and qualified as an alternate in my senior year. Near the end of my senior year, the NSA offered me a job as an analyst, so I graduated school and the next day moved to Fort Meade and went to work for the NSA."

The waitress brought back the ticket. Diane waited for Jack to finish as he figured out the tip and signed off on it. She had only known Jack a very short time, but she already liked him. She didn't want him to think she was bragging. No doubt he had left out some major accomplishments in the little biography he had given her.

She stood up and slipped on her jacket. "I'm sure my dad had something to do with me getting the job. Anyway, I have been with the NSA for the last six years. I was told this field assignment would look good on my resume," she said with a smirk on her face. "That is, if it doesn't kill me." She laughed.

"This job will probably bore you to death first," Jack countered and they both laughed.

They found the bumper stickers they wanted at the truck stop. Jack grinned when he found one that read, 'Back Off, I'm Not That Kind of Car.'

Diane's rose-colored glass beads hung on the rearview

mirror as she drove westbound on Interstate 70, the last leg to Columbus, Ohio. Jack was dozing in the passenger seat. She tapped her fingers on the steering wheel to the beat on the radio. She was enjoying driving the Suburban, but it was really slow compared to her Mustang. Getting bored, she called Katia and her dad and gave them quick updates on her day.

Jack woke slowly, stretched. "We should be getting close to Columbus."

"Almost there, sleepyhead." She pointed to an interstate sign–Columbus, Sixteen Miles.

They decided to stop for the night. Jack located a place right off Interstate 70, called the Buckeye Inn, and reserved two rooms.

"How many miles did you say to the Buckeye Inn?" Diane asked.

"Four or five. It should be right off the next exit."

"If you don't mind, I would like to pull over and run the rest of the way if you can take over the driving. I'll call you when I'm just about there."

Jack stretched and nodded. "I can do that."

Diane pulled over to the side of the road.

"Okay," Jack reached behind her seat and pulled out her Glock 22. "Tuck this in your belt. You can't be too careful."

Diane rolled her eyes. "Okay, old-timer. See you in a few." She began the short run toward the hotel.

A few minutes later Jack checked into the hotel with suitcases, laptops, and keys in hand. He placed Diane's suitcases just inside her door. Back in his room, he tossed his suitcase on the bed, then turned on the TV to WWN news. He dialed Diane. "Hey, how does a pizza sound?"

"Great. I'm just coming up to the parking lot."

"You're in room 1018 and I'm in room 1016. Come on up and get your key."

"Okay, but I need to shower as soon as possible."

"I'll call in a pizza. What do you like?"

"Anything but anchovies."

A short time later they were eating their pizza and going over the data from their laptops.

"When it comes to Compton, I have a gut feeling we are not talking about the city in California or in the U.K. Have you looked at any persons named Compton?" Jack asked.

"Yes, I have. The only name of any importance is Arthur H. Compton, a physicist from 1892 to 1962. In 1922, he confirmed the dual nature of electromagnetic radiation as both a wave and as a particle, now called the 'Compton Effect.' During the war, in 1942, he was head of the Manhattan Project's metallurgical laboratory. He was responsible for producing nuclear reactors to convert uranium into plutonium, finding ways to separate the plutonium from the uranium, and designing the atomic bomb. His theories help explain how an EMP nuclear weapon works by flooding electrons over the earth's magnetic field, destroying all electronics in its path."

"This is one of the things that scares me the most, Diane." Jack leaned over his laptop. "There was a study done on an attack like this back in 2004 and it stated an EMP bomb, detonated over America at a height of three hundred miles, would take down the national electric power grid, causing widespread civil unrest."

"No power would mean losing electricity, and that would lead to no water or sewage," Diane said with a frown.

"Yes, and we have more than three hundred and twenty million guns in America," Jack said with a sigh. It was a figure he had memorized. "It would turn into the Wild West, with everyone out for themselves. It would be like Katrina on a massive scale. Food would be off the store shelves in two days. Anyone who had food or water would become a target."

Diane could see where he was going with this. She had played out scenarios like this in her college sociology classes. "No trans- portation, because most cars and trucks have electronics in them and wouldn't work. Heating and cooling systems would go down… Planes in the sky would plummet and crash."

Jack sighed again. It was his worst nightmare. "Most deaths would occur in the first two weeks, and after the first year the population in America would be pre-1492, or about thirty-three million. So, we could be talking about three hundred million casualties. All from one nuclear bomb. The defense department fears an EMP attack might come from a missile fired from a freighter just off the east or west coasts."

"Wouldn't any country trying to do this be destroyed just after the missile reached us?"

"Yes, by our twelve Trident nuclear subs, each packing twenty-four missiles. We have over eighty military bases around the world, just for that reason."

"But a terrorist has no country to strike back against," Diane offered up her opinion.

"And therein lies the problem with EMPs. The perfect weapon of mass destruction for a terrorist. Now you know why Compton is a keyword of interest. And Blackbird, maybe, is a code word for a missile that brings darkness."

"Is that what Homeland Security thinks, Jack?" she asked.

"No, that's what I think it means. Just thinking out loud." Jack closed his laptop. "Get a good night's rest, Princess

Warrior, tomorrow we invade West Fifth Street."

"You want to meet up for breakfast in the morning around seven or seven thirty?"

"Sounds good," he replied.

"Sleep tight, and don't let the bedbugs bite," she teased.

"Damn, you would have to say that right before it's time for bed." He frowned at the thought of little critters in his bed.

"I hear they are as big as buckeyes, those zombie bed bugs," she said as she headed for the door.

"Goodnight."

"Goodnight, Jack."

Jack closed and locked the door behind her. *I think I may have met my match with this one. I'll have to make an effort not to let her or her father distract me from the mission. I must admit, this should be interesting.*

CHAPTER 6

June 27 at 7:35 a.m.

"GOOD MORNING, JACK," she said with a smile.

"Ready to save the world, Princess Warrior?" he asked.

"Today is as good as any." Diane beamed.

Jack waved her into his room. "I'll be ready in a minute." He went to the mirror in the bathroom to finish tying his tie. "I spoke to Max this morning, and we have an address for one Izad Jahandar at 216 West Fifth Street, Apartment H. Our mission is to get into his computer without him realizing he's being hacked. We need to go case the area. But first, can you run a search on him and tell me if he is married and if he is employed?"

"Sure, give me a few minutes." Diane went to the table and opened her laptop.

Jack came out, tie in place and slipping on his coat. "Well, what did you find out about our suspect?"

"He is unemployed, on welfare and food stamps. He is single, as far as I can tell. No car registered in his name, no gun permits, and he uses the local cable company for TV and internet. There are no felonies charged against him."

"Sounds perfect for a homegrown type of profile to me," Jack concluded.

Jack drove the Suburban out of the hotel parking lot. It was your typical summer day in central Ohio, seventy-eight degrees, a slight breeze, and beautiful. It didn't take long before they were on West 5th, a street lined on both sides with maple trees and older two-story red brick apartment buildings. A bar and restaurant were situated at the intersection. Jack turned down Greentree, one block away from where the suspect lived. He spotted an alley half a block away and pulled in to park the Suburban. He could barely see the Izad apartment building from the alley.

"You stick around and guard the Suburban. I want to walk around the block and determine what we have here. Just for the hell of it, search the wi-fi routers in the area and see if any of them are unsecured, okay?" Jack asked.

"Roger that. Be careful."

Jack began walking down the sidewalk toward Izad's apartment building. He loved the summer, with its warm breezes and the smell of fresh cut grass. He took note of two kids playing basketball across the street. It reminded him of his youth in Indiana, when he played basketball with his friends. He took basketball very seriously in those days, and so did his buddies.

A few cars passed by as he got closer. He noticed a single door in the front of the apartment building that he imagined must be a common entrance to the building. With no call button or intercom, the door must always remain unlocked.

Jack entered the apartment building. On his left were eight recessed mailboxes in the wall, with names above them. As he scanned the mailboxes, he saw Box H had Izad's name above it. He also noted the box above belonged to Mary Caylor. He proceeded down the hallway. There were two apartments on the left and two on the right. All the doors were metal and marked with a three-inch letter under their peepholes.

THE BLACKBIRD THREAT

At the end of the hallway was a staircase that led upstairs. Jack walked up the creaky wooden stairs to the second floor. It was only a short distance to Apartment E, across the hall from H. He listened for sounds of voices, TV, or radio at each of the apartment doors. There was no sound coming from Apartment E, but he heard music from what they'd been told was Izad's apartment. He paused to think.

Diane was having difficulty finding a wi-fi router that was unsecured. She sighed with exasperation and looked in the direction Jack had headed. No telling when he would return.

She checked her email. There was one from Katia. As she was reading that message, she heard a tap on the window. She looked up to see a young black man standing beside the door, pointing a pistol at her head.

The man yelled, "Get out of the car or I'll blow your damn head off!"

Diane slowly opened the door. "What are you doing? Carjacking us?"

"Who else is with you?" he asked.

"My dad, and he'll be back soon."

"Give me the keys right now if you want to live," the man threatened. His voice quavered and the pistol in his hand shook.

He was either new to carjacking or on drugs. In any case, Diane didn't want any trouble.

"I don't have the key. It's one of those with a push-button start. My dad has the key fob with him. Just walk away. I won't tell anyone about this, I promise," Diane advised him in a steady tone. They were supposed to be doing this investigation covertly. They did not need an incident that the local police would be pulled into.

She stood facing the man with her back against the passenger door. She estimated he was five feet ten inches and about a hundred and seventy pounds. He stood inches from her face. She could smell his breath and took note of a scar on the left side of his forehead and a gold front tooth.

The man pointed his pistol at her head.

Jack appeared from around the corner of the building in the alley with his Glock in hand. "Drop the gun!" he demanded in an official tone.

Diane took advantage of the startled man as he glanced in Jack's direction. She quickly lunged and grabbed the pistol with her left hand. At the same time, using a front snap kick, she placed her foot in the man's groin. As he moaned and crouched forward, Diane brought her knee up under his chin and her clasped fist down on the back of his head, driving it into her knee, this time breaking his nose. She reached over with her right hand and pushed his gun's magazine release button, causing it to fall to the pavement. She quickly slammed her right hand down on his extended arm, then gave him a chop to the throat. He dropped the gun, clutching at his nose. Diane kicked the gun away. It spun and landed in front of the Suburban.

Jack calmly walked up to her. "I don't know what you would do without me." He turned toward the carjacker. "Face down! Hands behind your back!"

Diane retrieved a set of handcuffs from the glove compartment. She put her knee on the small of his back and cuffed him.

Never had a chance to do this except in a simulation, Diane thought. *It probably gets easier with a little bit of practice.*

Jack and Diane lifted the carjacker to his feet. They put him in a seated position, with his back against the red brick building on the corner of the alley.

Jack smiled at him. "Dude, not exactly your lucky day, is it? You just tried to commit an armed robbery and assaulted a federal agent. And you just got your ass kicked by a girl! You are lucky she didn't kill you!"

"Aww, thank you, Jack. That is very sweet of you to say."

"Anytime, Princess," Jack replied. "Do you have an ID, Mr. Carjacker?" he asked.

"I'm Jerry Butler. I wasn't gonna hurt anybody. I's just gonna take the SUV to make some fast money, man. I got an old lady and kids to feed."

Jack gave the guy a smug look. "Jerry, do you have a picture of your kids?"

"In my billfold."

Jack leaned over and removed his billfold from his back pocket. He opened it and found Jerry's driver's license, two one-dollar bills, and a picture of three young kids.

Blood was running from Jerry's nose, down over his chin, and onto his faded gray Cleveland Cavaliers tee shirt. His left eye was swollen almost shut.

Jack showed Diane the picture of Jerry's kids. He grabbed Jerry and dragged him back into the alley in front of the Suburban. "Jerry, do you know anyone that lives in that building over there?" Jack pointed to Izad's unit.

"No, sir, I don't."

"Good answer," replied Jack.

Diane helped Jack drag Jerry back into the alley beside the Suburban and lean him back up against the wall.

Jack walked over and sat down in the passenger seat with the door open, facing Jerry. "Have you ever seen the show *Let's Make a Deal*?"

Jerry nodded his head.

"Well then, let's play." Jack reached into his pocket. "I really like your gun, Jerry. I'll give you three hundred dollars for your gun. Or you can keep it, and go straight to jail."

"I'll take the money," Jerry replied without hesitation.

"Good, and now for part two of the deal." Jack reached behind the seat and pulled out one of the HK MP7 submachine guns, then locked and loaded a twenty-round magazine and pointed the gun at Jerry. "You are a big distraction to my work, Jerry Butler. You need to go away for good." Jack took a very long hard glaring look at Jerry. "Here's the deal... if I see you again, I will put these twenty bullets in you. You do not take one step into this street for a year. Or, I can read you your rights and you can go straight to jail. What's it going to be?"

"You won't ever see me again," Jerry moaned.

"Good," replied Jack with a satisfied smirk.

He walked over to Jerry and unlocked the handcuffs, then handed Jerry three one-hundred-dollar bills. "Go buy your kids some food and go to the doctor and have him fix your damn nose. Here is today's tip: Get a damn job! Carjacking is not a job, dumbass. It's a crime! Stop doing this shit and get a life. Do it for your kids. Your kids deserve better, man up!"

After a long pause, Jack told him, "Have a nice life with your kids, Jerry Butler. Now get the hell out of here and leave us alone!"

"Yes, sir, and thank you," Jerry said as he hustled down the alley, wiping the blood from his face and not looking back.

"What the hell just happened, Jack? Why did you let him go?"

"Three reasons, Diane. First, he is not a terrorist; he's just a desperate street thug. Second, you made his face into a total mess, so his lawyer would sue Homeland Security and/or the

Columbus Police Department for police brutality. And third, I don't want to come back here for a court appearance this year or next year. Do you?"

"No, no way," she had to admit.

"And now I'm adding a fourth reason. That gun is worth every bit of five hundred dollars. And I just got a gun off the street from a thug. I will have the FBI check the ballistics just to make sure it's clean."

"I guess if the gun was pointed at your head, you might feel a little different about turning him loose!" Diane said.

"Maybe, but you must look at the big picture here, Diane. I'm trying to protect three hundred forty million Americans from a terrorist attack, not play cops. We need to keep a very low profile. As invisible as possible."

"Right. I get it." She had just lost track of the issues when that gun was pointed at her head.

Jack walked over to the driver's side of the car and opened the door. "Let's go get a cup of coffee. I have an idea of how we can accomplish our mission here."

Jack and Diane found a coffee shop a block away. She made a trip to the restroom and washed the blood from Jerry's face off her hands and pant leg. When she got back to the table, Jack explained his position on the ease of conning the truth out of someone rather than beating it out of them.

Two cups of coffee and a slice of apple pie later, Jack and Diane had come up with a plan.

CHAPTER 7

THEY RETURNED TO the hotel after stopping by an office supply store. Diane purchased several flash drives.

Jack bought a printer and an AC inverter so he could charge the laptops in the Suburban and print documents while on the road. Jack called Max to make sure Homeland Security had a search warrant out for Izad Jahandar. He described the plan in detail to Max, and Max gave Jack the thumbs-up to go ahead.

Diane emailed Katia and told her to run a three-hop search on Izad's social media accounts, if he had any.

A three-hop search was conducted, starting with everyone in Izad's email and social media contacts list, which was hop one. Then a search was conducted on everyone they had in *their* contact lists–hop two–and then, finally, everyone *they* had contact with, hop three. This type of search gave a total of three levels of possible connections, and up to as many as a million personal contacts. The computer algorithms began looking for common persons, locations, and/or events.

Diane's ringtone sounded. "Hi, Katia."

"Hi, Diane, I hate to ask you this, but can I borrow your car so I can see my aunt in Chicago? She is my only relative living in America and is the one who walked across Russia with my mother and me. She has cancer and wants to see me before she dies. Of course, I said I will. I don't think the Kat-mobile will make it there and back. I'm scared to death I'll break down on the highway."

"Yes, by all means, take my car. In my apartment, under my mattress, I have a Sig Sauer 226 pistol my dad gave me as a high school graduation gift. Just be careful, I keep it loaded and there is a round in the chamber."

"Oh, thanks, sweetie. I'm not sure about taking the pistol. I don't have a concealed carry permit."

"Just take it, I want you to feel safe traveling alone, you can just leave it in the car."

"Oh, by the way, today we received a new upgrade on a hacking software. I know it will work on your laptop. I would send you a link, but I'm not allowed to risk sending it on the internet. I can make a copy on a thumb drive and hand-deliver it to you if you are near Chicago. What do you think?"

"Sounds good. We will be in Dearborn soon. I think every little bit helps."

"Okay, I'll make the copy. And thanks again, sweetie, you are like the little sister I never had."

"I feel the same way about you, K. I'm so sorry to hear about your aunt."

"Well, my break time is over, I'd better get back to work… or you-know-who will find me," she laughed. "Call you later. Love you, Diane, bye."

"Bye, K."

"It's nice to see that you have a coworker like Katia," Jack said.

"She's my work angel. I remember my first day working at the NSA, pulling into the parking lot. There must have been twenty thousand cars. I was so intimidated and a little scared; she said, 'Relax, you work at one of the safest facilities in the world, my friend.'"

Jack was investigating persons living in the same apartment

building as Izad. He started with Mary Caylor in apartment A and Rick Reed in apartment E. Mary was a cook at Lakeside Hospital and Rick worked for an engineering company. Both worked during the day. Mary had lived in her apartment for two years, and Rick had been there just over a month. That was perfect for Jack's plan.

Diane was getting ready to pay a visit to Izad. She put her long blonde hair up in a ponytail. She threw on an Ohio State tee shirt. She purchased the shirt at a clothing store near the Ohio State campus just minutes before. She called Jack's room. "Ready whenever you are."

"Well then, let's roll, Diane," he replied.

Sixteen minutes later they were sitting in the Suburban they'd parked in the bar parking lot near Izad's apartment building. Jack took the flash drive, Diane downloaded top-secret spying software, along with a porn movie, and wrote 'Private RR' on it.

He stepped out of the vehicle and dragged the flash drive on the cement sidewalk. As he was walking back to the SUV, he reached behind the left front tire and rubbed his finger against the mud flap. He rubbed the dirt he collected on the flash drive and handed it to her. "All set. Just try not to beat him up, okay?"

Diane smiled. "You always say the sweetest things, Jack."

They both laughed.

"Okay, Diane, remember I will be at the bottom of the stairs if you need me."

"I got this, Double-Oh." Diane grinned.

She was wearing a mic that looked like an iPod. The idea was for her to record Izad's voice and make a voiceprint of him. Once a person's voiceprint was downloaded into the NSA databanks, they could scan thousands of cell phone calls per second to find and pinpoint the suspect's voice and location.

Jack tucked his gun into the waistband of his shorts, with his tee shirt hanging over the top. He followed Diane into the back entrance of the apartment building.

Jack was wearing a receiver, disguised as earbuds. He heard her take a deep breath as she walked up to apartment E and knocked very loudly on the door.

Diane was counting on Rick still being at work. After about thirty seconds, she took another deep breath, cleared her throat, and walked across the hall to apartment H.

She could hear the TV through the door. She knocked loudly on Izad's door.

Startled, he jumped from his recliner and picked up a twelve-inch kitchen carving knife from an end table. He came to the door and looked out the peephole.

He opened the door halfway, holding the knife in his right hand against the wall, head-high and out of Diane's sight. He leaned forward, sticking his head out into the hall. Relieved she was alone, he said, "Yes, what do you want?"

"Hi, my name is Karen Waters. My friends call me KJ. Anyway, I'm friends with Mary in apartment A. I came over to see her this morning and I saw this man drop something as he was leaving the building. So, I went over where he dropped it and found this flash drive thingy on the sidewalk. I picked it up and showed it to Mary.

"Mary told me it belongs to Rick Reed, who is the guy that lives above her and across from you." She leaned into the door frame, letting him get a good look at her cleavage. "She told me that he's a perv. She hears porn and stuff coming from his apartment all the time and it's very annoying. When I told Mary we should give it to him when he comes home from work, she said she wanted nothing to do with him and to just throw it out. But later I got to thinking that it might not be porn but something work-related and he'd want it back. He's still not home, so can you give it to him? Or if you don't want to then just throw it away. I don't have time to wait around, mister…?"

"Izad. Yes, I will take care of it for you." He smiled and for a second, he fantasized about plunging the knife into her neck and watching her die in his arms after he had his way with her.

She held her hand out straight with the flash drive in her palm. He reached for the drive and dragged his fingers slowly from the back of her palm to the ends of her fingertips, then snatched up the drive in one stroke.

Okay, that was creepy. One more move and it's time to kick this dude's ass. "Thank you so much. You're kind of sweet and cute. Maybe I'll see you around sometime." She gave him a big smile and a slow wink.

"That would be nice. I will be looking forward to it," he said in his thick Arabic accent.

"Thanks again, hon," she replied with a flirty look. She turned away and sashayed down the hall, turning her head for a quick look over her shoulder to make sure he wasn't sneaking up on her on the way to the stairs.

Izad watched her strut to the end of the hall and then he closed and locked the door.

Jack met Diane at the bottom of the stairs. "Well done. Let's go back to the hotel and see if he takes the bait."

Once they were back in the SUV, Diane flipped open her laptop. She logged on and stated triumphantly, "There he is. We got him!"

"Awesome! These scumbags are so predictable. Okay,

copy everything on his hard drive–we need all his emails, contacts, friends lists, and browsing history."

"I should have it by the time we get back to the hotel," Diane replied.

"Great, I'll email Max and let him know we're in."

CHAPTER 8

Buckeye Inn, Columbus, Ohio
Room 1016

JACK EMAILED MAX and informed him Diane was now following protocol and scanning Izad's hard drive and all his emails. They should be able to forward the results tonight or first thing in the morning. Max replied that he was pleased with their progress, and encouraged them to keep going. He also reminded them they were to be in Dearborn tomorrow. He would give them all the details when they arrived.

Jack called Diane. "Hey, how's it going? I need you to pull all the emails from his computer with an IP address for any persons living in the Dearborn area. Max has us headed that way tomorrow. I have laundry to do, and I'm ordering out Chinese. You want me to order any for you?"

"Laundry, already? You didn't pack enough clothes." Jack could hear the tease in her voice. "No thanks, I'm in the mood for a salad. Besides, I'll be up most of the night breaking down the results for Max. Have a good night."

"You too, Diane. See you in the morning, around seven?"

"Roger that, goodnight."

Forty minutes later, Jack was sitting on the bed in his hotel room, eating his Chinese food and watching the Worldwide News channel on a small TV sitting on an old dark oak dresser. The news reporter was warning of an increase in terrorist activity as a possibility throughout the Fourth of July holiday.

In other news, the recent launch of a weather satellite by the Iranian Space Agency appeared to be in trouble, as the satellite's orbit was decaying. Scientists predicted its fall to Earth within days or weeks. The State Department had received a "No comment" from the Iranian government on the condition of the satellite.

I wonder if the satellite has a role in the Blackbird threat?

Jack remembered the briefing discussing an EMP attack, where just one nuclear device could take down the national electric grid in America, and most of Canada and Mexico. He went to bed with a bad feeling in his gut that something was about to happen.

* * *

Diane took in a deep sigh and closed her laptop after finishing several computer programs dissecting Izad's information copied from his computer. Lying in her bed, she called Katia and told her about the attempted carjacking and how easy it was to trick Izad and gain access to his computer.

"Oh, my God, Diane, you could have been killed this morning!"

It was at this moment the events of the day hit Diane. "Maybe you could say a prayer for me, Katia? I feel like I'm in a little over my head with these covert operations."

Katia could hear the stress and the anxiety she was feeling in her voice. She attempted to give some reassurance and raise her friend's spirits. "Diane... Sweetie... the whole department is very proud of you. You are the bravest and strongest person I know. I almost feel sorry for anyone who comes up against you."

"Thanks, K. I'll be going to Dearborn, Michigan tomorrow. Wish me luck!"

"Call me tomorrow night. Love you, my friend."

"Love you too. Goodnight."

Diane plugged her cell into the charger, turned out the light, and tried to get some sleep.

Jack's room phone rang with his 6:00 a.m. wake-up call. With the phone still in his hand, he called Diane. "Good morning, Princess. You ready to save the world?"

"Not before I have an extra-large coffee."

"Deal! I'll meet you down in the lobby in an hour, okay?"

"That's doable," she replied.

"I have a surprise for you. I'll see you in a few. Bye."

Jack met Diane in the lobby and handed her a large coffee. "I already have us checked out. They just need your room key."

"Cool, okay. What's the surprise?"

"We are stopping at my house, so I can pick up some more clothes and a few toys. You up for a little target practice?"

"Sure, what weapons are we firing?"

"Well, first I want to zero in my sights on my HK MP7. I have never fired one of these before."

"Me neither. I could use some practice too," she agreed.

After grabbing a quick bite to eat, they started traveling west on Interstate 70, toward Indiana. "I just live two-and-a-half hours from here. We can still make Dearborn by tonight. Have you ever been to Indiana?"

"No, that is one of the few states I've missed," she said and smiled.

Her sitting there with her large crystal blue eyes reminded him of the time he took his twelve-year-old daughter to Disneyland many years ago, during one of his few happier times.

"Well, Princess, Indiana is mostly flat with trees and farmland, corn and soybean fields, and small towns. Low-cost housing and family values make it a nice place to raise a family."

"That's nice. Jack, I don't mind you calling me Princess, or Princess Warrior, because you got that from my dad–just remember, this princess can kick your ass if necessary!" Her face turned bright red as she gave Jack an ice-cold stare.

"Whoa, Diane, I'm sorry if you thought I was mocking you! I always give people I like and respect nicknames. It's kind of my thing, you know? And it fits you so well."

"Just saying, Jack."

"Duly noted," Jack shot back.

Neither one spoke a word for the next fifty miles.

Finally, Diane asked, "Have you ever been married?"

"I got married when I was in college, and we had a baby girl a year later. I thought everything was great, but by then I had a growing drinking problem. My wife wouldn't put up with me. I didn't really blame her. I was not easy to live with. This was going on at the same time I was struggling to teach history to a bunch of kids who didn't give a damn about the subject. Or it may have been because their teacher had terrible hangovers." Jack kept his eyes on the road as a frown creased his forehead. "So, by the time I enlisted in the army, she'd had enough and divorced me. She wanted nothing to do with me. I burned every bridge in my marriage, so I haven't seen my daughter in over twenty-five years. To make matters worse, I became a grandpa a couple years ago, but I have yet to see my grandson."

"Wow, that's pretty sad. Do you think you can ever patch things up with your daughter?"

"I don't know. I'm not the same man as she has in her memories. I don't drink anymore. I haven't touched a drop in twenty years. I called her a few times, but she would never pick up. I would leave a message on the answering machine telling her I was sorry, and I would always love her and my grandson. She never returned my calls. I hope someday she may have a change of heart, but I'm not counting on it. What about you, Princess—I mean, Diane?"

Diane giggled. "It's all right, Jack—I mean, Mike." She smiled and gave him her patented princess hand wave.

Jack smiled back. "Okay, you win, Diane... this time."

"To answer your question, or should I say confession, I was nearly engaged once. Wayne was a senior, and I was a junior at Georgia Tech. He was a finance major and a sweet guy, very handsome and a Southern Gentleman. Even my dad liked him. His parents were millionaires. His life was set even before graduating from college. Only one problem between us–he wanted a lot of children."

Diane took a deep breath and went on. "I wanted to make a name for myself and be of service to my country. I didn't want to be a baby momma. I felt my life was meant to be something more than a mother and a housewife. I guess it's a DNA thing. So, we went our separate ways.

"I know a lot of women dream of being set for life, living in a large house on the hill, and raising a large family, but it just wasn't my dream. That kind of life seemed like a nightmare to me."

"What *is* your life's dream?"

"Long-term... I really... I am not sure, but for now, I am living the dream. I have an important job, great friends, a nice car, and an apartment. What more could a girl want?"

Jack nodded his head in agreement and rubbed his sore neck. "Well, for a twenty-eight-year-old, you do seem to have it together."

The two-hour drive passed quickly, and Jack was pulling into his driveway. "Come on in. I want to show you my safe room. The most secret CIA headquarters in Indiana. Only three people have ever seen it."

Diane wondered, *What the hell? This I have to see.* She followed him into his home and was surprised at how nice and tidy everything looked.

"Down the hall and the first door on your left is a coat closet." He opened the closet door and shoved the coats to one side. He ran his hand down the wall until she heard a loud click and the back wall swung open into his safe room.

"How does that work, Jack?" Diane asked with a puzzled look.

"I have an RFID chip implanted in my hand. Only I can unlock the door." Jack motioned her to enter. "Go on in, I need to grab a few more shirts from my bedroom."

Diane went down the steps into the safe room. Before she could even search for a light switch, the lights came on automatically.

The room was about twenty feet long and twelve feet wide, loaded with weapons and equipped with a computer and ham radio. A small bed was located in the corner. There was a bathroom stall with floor-to-ceiling walls but no door. It had a sink and toilet on one wall and a shower on the other. It was only about four-foot square. On the other side of the wall was the small bed, with a mini fridge next to it doubling as a nightstand.

Jack stuck his head in the door. "Do you feel safe in here?

Twelve inches of reinforced concrete and steel walls, ceiling, and floor. It has a trapdoor and a two-hundred-foot tunnel to the outside world."

"What the hell, Jack, who are you expecting? Who did you piss off?" she asked.

"While working for the CIA, I managed to piss off quite a few people," Jack boasted.

"Which side, ours or theirs?" she joked.

"Both. I was an overachiever! I was in the Boy Scouts. You know their motto, and I am *always* prepared.

"I want to take a little more firepower with us, just in case. Have you ever fired one of these?" He held up an M60 machine gun. "This one is a little surplus left over from the Vietnam War."

"Nope, but I can't wait to try out this puppy," she said with a big grin.

"I'm going to call my friend and see if we can have the shooting range to ourselves for about thirty minutes."

"That would be awesome. You can do that?" Diane questioned.

Jack chuckled. "It helps if you are a federal agent and on the board of directors of the local shooting range." He grabbed a couple of smoke grenades, a roll of duct tape, and a medic first aid kit. "Hey, have you ever flown one of these quadcopter drones?"

"No, I haven't, but I've always wanted to."

"We will take it with us. It has an HD camera and transmits the video to my phone. You never know when you need an eye in the sky." He winked in a conspiratorial way.

Twenty minutes later they were on the shooting range. Jack showed Diane how to load the ammo belt into the M60. She fired the machine gun at an old Ford pickup truck six hundred meters away.

Jack flew the drone down to look at her targets on the old truck. "Well done, Princess. The truck is just riddled with holes."

After shooting all their weapons, the pair got back in the Suburban and headed north to Dearborn, taking Interstate 69 in northern Indiana. Jack was estimating arriving around 6:00 p.m.

CHAPTER 9

JACK SLOWED DOWN and took the next exit. "Nature is calling. Do you need anything? I'm going to gas up at this truck stop."

Lightning flashed off to the north as the Suburban rolled to a stop beside the gas pumps.

"Yes, I have to go too. My tank is way past full," she said as she got out of the SUV. "I'm grabbing some coffee. Do you want any?"

"Nah, I think I'll get something cold. I'll meet you inside."

He pumped gas into the tank, then walked into the truck stop to the dark-haired girl running the register. "Could you recommend a good hotel or motel in Dearborn?"

"No, I never go there anymore, not since those foreigners took over half the city."

"Well, I can understand that," he replied. Jack grabbed a big bag of chips and a large Coke to add to the gas bill.

Diane was looking in a big display box of discounted music CDs. "Hey, Jack, do you like Guns N' Roses?"

"Oh yeah, who doesn't? I like 'Sweet Child of Mine.'"

"You rock, Jack. That's one of my favorite songs of all time!" Diane fist bumped him when she brought the CD up to the register. "Put this on his bill."

A few minutes later, Diane began driving the last leg to Dearborn as a late afternoon thunderstorm moved through the area and classic rock boomed from the radio speakers. They were in a good mood, but in the back of their minds, neither one knew what the near future held.

Diane received a call from Katia.

"Do you need anything from your apartment?"

"No, I'm in good shape right now. I look forward to seeing you. I miss you, Katia."

"I miss you too."

They both sighed as they hung up.

* * *

6:18 p.m.
Dearborn, Michigan

"Okay, Princess, take a left on Ford Road. We need to get you some clothes, so you can blend in here in Dearborn. There is a mall or a shopping center a couple of miles ahead. The road turns into a one-way highway."

"Roger that, old-timer," she laughed. "What is it I am morphing into?"

"We will be going into some Muslim neighborhoods. I don't think there are many blonde-haired, blue-eyed ladies. And you may want to pick up a dark eyebrow pencil too. The hijab should cover your hair."

"I feel like a Hollywood actress going on the set."

"Yes, that about sums it up, all right. Except I don't see any Oscars coming your way and your critics here can, and will, kill you," Jack emphasized.

"Well then, I'd better put on the performance of a lifetime." Diane hung a left on Ford.

"There's a clothing store. Pull in here." Jack pointed toward an empty parking space. "It has been a while since I was in the Middle East. I believe a dress is called an *abaya*, and a headscarf is called a hijab. If anyone asks, okay?"

"Okay, Captain Jack."

Once inside the store, a Muslim lady in a full, dark blue headscarf and matching dress with white trim welcomed them. "Can I help you with anything? We have a sixty percent off sale on those racks with the red tags near the back wall."

"We are just looking, thank you," answered Diane.

After a half hour of browsing, Diane picked out a black *abaya* with gold trim and matching hijab. Diane paid for her clothes and complimented the woman on her store.

The Muslim lady walked them to the door and waved good-bye. She took a picture of them with her iPhone as they got in their SUV and then made a call. "Good evening. I just had a couple in my store. An older man and a young blonde woman. He was coaching her on Muslim etiquette. They bought a black *abaya* and a matching hijab. They paid with a government credit card. I thought you should know. They were driving a new black Suburban. I care about you!"

"Thank you, Venya, we will be fine. God is with us," the man on the other end said.

Diane and Jack spotted a nice hotel. They pulled into the parking lot just as Jack received a call from Max.

"Jack, are you in Dearborn yet?"

"Just arrived."

"We have a situation with another team. Agents Doug Dickinson and Joe Thomas are not far from you. They are requesting back-up immediately! They have active shooters at their location. They're about six miles out of Dearborn. I'll send you the address and a link to an unarmed drone video feed so you can locate them! I'll patch you into a conference call, you can talk to them over the SUV's speakerphone. Be careful, Jack!"

Diane flipped open her laptop. "Got it!"

"We're on it, Max. Tell them to hang on," Jack responded.

Adrenaline surged through their veins.

Jack threw the SUV into reverse. "Grab the bulletproof vests, and lock and load all the weapons."

At the same time, Jack called 9-1-1. "This is Jack Jacobs of Homeland Security. We have a Level Red event happening on county road 600 West. I need the Dearborn SWAT team on standby at the corner of 600 West and Rangeline roads, now! And the Michigan State Police must clear out all traffic in that area! We have personnel on location and engaged with multiple active shooters. This is a terrorist event. Please call your local Homeland Security director and give him my number, thank you."

He glanced at Diane as they sped down the road. "I bet that was a new one for that nine-one-one call center." Jack was flying down the street at seventy-five miles per hour with emergency flashers on and honking the horn as traffic scrambled to get out of the way. Diane was shouting directions to Jack from the GPS on her cell phone.

Jack noticed, in the rearview mirror, police cars were falling in behind him but having trouble keeping up. "Hey, can you call nine-one-one again and request a police escort in front of us, instead of behind? They're not helping much back there. Give them the directions we are following!"

"Done. I already texted them the directions," she replied.

"You really are a princess warrior! Now send the police the video feed link so they can see, in real time, what is happening."

"Roger that, Captain Jack."

Jack was driving with one eye on the road and one eye on the drone's video feed, coming from high above the two-story farmhouse that was visible on Diane's laptop.

"We are about one minute from the scene," she informed him.

"What is that behind the house, a shed or garage?" he asked.

"I'm not sure, but I saw a man running into it. He's still in there."

"Agent Dickinson, this is Agent Jack Jacobs and Agent Diane Glass. Our ETA is thirty seconds. Do you have someone in the building behind the house?"

"No, the two of us are pinned down behind our vehicle. Two shooters, one in the top left window facing us and another at the downstairs window near the front door," answered Agent Doug Dickinson.

Jack had known Doug a little over three years. They'd worked a few investigations together. "Doug, we saw a man run into the building behind the house on the drone's feed. We will engage the suspect in the outbuilding first and then join you."

"Right on, my friend," Doug replied.

As they drove up to the farmhouse, Diane could see their Suburban come into the picture on the video feed.

Jack slowed down. "Diane, get your window down and be ready to take a shot if needed."

Driving fast, Jack jerked the wheel and the Suburban bounced over a small ditch and into a wet grassy area, slinging mud beside the house, going toward the outbuilding. A man suddenly sprang from the building and ran toward their truck at full speed.

Jack yelled, "Take the shot, take the shot!"

Diane leaned way out the window with her HK MP7 and fired two quick shots, stopping the guy cold. Jack jerked hard on Diane's arm, pulling her back inside the Suburban just before a giant explosion rocked the vehicle. It almost overturned the SUV. Regaining control, Jack floored it while turning the steering wheel sharply to the left and engaging the emergency brake, causing the SUV to spin ninety degrees on the wet grass and stop parallel to the building. Diane jumped out and secured the back corner of the building as Jack scooped up his HK MP7 submachine gun and darted out the backseat passenger door. Jack signaled Diane to go around the building and meet him at the door.

Diane's heart was racing so fast it felt like it would jump out of her chest at any moment. Smoke was hanging in the air, making visibility difficult. The smell of gunpowder surrounded her, and her ears were ringing from the suicide bomber's explosion.

This must be what my dad felt like during a battle. She slowly moved around the building until she met Jack at the open door. She was on one side and he on the other. Jack hand-signaled to her that they would go in on the count of three, and for her to stay low. *One... two... three...* They both pivoted into the doorway. Jack stood up and Diane crouched low. The red dots from their laser scopes danced on the dark back wall of the building. The building was empty except for workbenches with timers and a few other electronic parts scattered about, along with short sections of pipe. It was obvious they were making bombs back here.

Jack called to Dickinson, "Scratch one bad guy, rear building secure!

"Diane, you stay here and guard the back of the house. I'm going to help take out that son of a bitch. Call me. Keep it on speakerphone and I'll do the same."

"Be careful!"

Jack jumped back in the Suburban and sped out across the backyard of the farmhouse. Shots rang out from inside the back door. Jack stomped on the gas pedal to move out of the shooter's line of fire.

Diane saw the muzzle flash and returned fire in the direction of the shooter.

Jack drove around to the front of the house and slid the SUV up against the bumper of Agent Dickinson's vehicle, trying to create more cover. Jack climbed over the console, stepped outside the passenger side rear door, and reached back for his M60 machine gun and a hundred-round ammo belt. He crouched low until he came to rest with his back against the rear tire.

Jack looked over to Doug. "How are you doing?"

"Oh, you know, I've been better. But it's just another day at the office with someone trying to shoot my ass," Doug replied sarcastically.

"Just like the old days. No one said saving the world would be easy, Doug!" Jack yelled. "Diane, are you okay?"

"Yes, no movement detected and all quiet in the back of the house."

"Copy that, Princess Warrior," Jack ack-nowledged.

"Who the hell is your partner, Xena or Wonder Woman?" Doug asked.

"Oh, you'll be amazed," Jack replied.

The upstairs shooter trained his gun in Jack's direction. Bullets sprayed down on the Suburban from the shooter's AK-47. He stopped to reload

Jack shouted, "He's reloading!" He jumped up with the M60 and fired all one hundred rounds from his ammo belt.

Agents Dickinson and Thomas also returned fire. Not much was standing around the upstairs window. Large holes riddled the walls and glass tinkled to the ground everywhere. The pink wall insulation littered the ground. When it all stopped, there was no one standing at the window.

"Well, what do you think… is he with his seventy-two virgins?" Doug asked.

Jack smirked. "Yeah, we got him. Now we need to get inside to get the intel before we can let the others clean up this mess. Diane, we are entering the house, hold your fire on any movement. Do you copy?" Jack requested.

"Got ya," Diane responded.

Jack motioned Dickson and Thomas into the SUV. He then drove across the front yard and stopped up against the porch. The agents scrambled out the Suburban's side door and up the steps. Jack opened the old wood-frame screen door while Doug slowly turned the front door knob. It wasn't locked, so Doug slowly pushed it open with the end of his M4 assault rifle.

Within there was only eerie silence. The sound of the door squeaking was a little unnerving. There was no sign of life in the living room, so the agents slowly entered the residence. Doug pointed to one dead terrorist, lying in a pool of blood on the kitchen floor near the back door. As they turned and slowly proceeded up the stairs, Doug was in the lead and was startled to see a woman and a small boy on the floor in the hallway. The woman and the boy were both alive, but the woman was bleeding from her side. The boy appeared unharmed. He was standing in front of the woman with his hand straight out as if to shield her from gunfire. He was not making a sound as tears ran down his face.

"You shot my mommy," he cried.

Jack peeked into the bedroom, where the other shooter was firing on them just seconds ago. He was lying face down on the floor, covered with blood and obviously dead. Empty shell casings were scattered about, and the smell of gunpowder was so strong he could taste it on his tongue. The other rooms upstairs were empty.

Jack gave Diane the all-clear and told her to start downloading the files from all computers and cell phones in the residence.

He called Max. "All secure here. We need an ambulance and the bomb squad. Three dead terrorists, one wounded female who is the mother of a young boy. Also, notify Child Protective Services for the boy. Diane is downloading all the data here; we will leave the computers intact for the FBI. We need the local SWAT team to secure the area until the bomb squad gives us the all clear. I'm thinking we need a news blackout or a cover story for at least a few days, no need to show that we are here."

"Excellent job, Jack," Max said. "I couldn't be prouder of both teams this evening."

Diane sat down and put her arm around the boy. "Your mother is going to be all right. Help is on the way."

Jack picked up the woman in the hallway and carried her downstairs, then outside to the porch. He laid her down and applied direct pressure to her wound.

"Was that your husband upstairs?"

"Yes, you killed him," she mumbled, with tears running down her cheeks.

"I'm so sorry this happened to you. Well, you have a big decision to make, don't you?" he said to her as he knelt beside her. "You can cooperate with the investigators and live a somewhat normal life. Or you can spend the rest of your life in prison. And a stranger will raise your son, and you'll watch your son grow up full of hate and die a violent death, the same as his father. The decision is yours."

She glared at Jack but said nothing.

Sirens wailed as the local police, SWAT team, and an ambulance arrived on the scene. The police recovered seven AK-47 assault rifles, thousands of rounds of ammunition, fourteen pipe bombs, and five suicide vests found under a mattress. After an hour and a half debriefing, Jack, Diane, Doug, and Joe left the scene for a late-night dinner. They settled for an Italian restaurant near Doug and Joe's hotel.

Diane enjoyed the meal and conversation between Jack and Doug as they talked about some cases they were involved in and people they had worked with over the years. They had some of the craziest war stories she had ever heard. She was not sure if it was the company or the three glasses of wine, but she was in a very good mood.

Jack noticed Doug couldn't keep his eyes off Diane. He couldn't blame him. After all, she was a beautiful young lady.

After dinner, Doug wrote his phone number and email address on a slip of paper and handed it to Diane. "Call me when the smoke clears and you're back in D.C.," Doug said with a smile.

"Sure, I can always use a cup of coffee." She smiled back.

After calling Max, they decided to hunker down at the same hotel and get their Suburbans repaired at the body shop. They did not need to call attention to themselves with all the bullet holes riddled in both Suburbans.

Jack and Doug were in luck, because the company that added the armor plating to the Suburbans was in nearby Detroit. A new high-impact bulletproof windshield and window glass, bodywork, and paint would require a minimum of three days to repair.

With no time to waste, Max decided he wanted Doug to interview the wife who was wounded and was now in the hospital under police guard. Thomas would do a background check on the three dead terrorists. Jack and Diane were ordered to go over contact lists and analyze all intel recovered from the farmhouse.

Diane did a three-hop search on the cell phones recovered and compiled a list of names and phone numbers that were in common. She then checked them against the list from the Columbus suspect, and the list from the old man in Syria.

Jack entered the common cell numbers into the Stingray cell phone processing unit that was now recording phone calls from those local numbers. No mention of the word Compton or Blackbird turned up.

Jack was worried. *Maybe we are following a dead-end?*

It had been three days since the firefight at the farmhouse. Jack called for a meeting with Doug, Tom, Diane, and a conference call with Max to disclose what the investigation had uncovered.

"Okay, Max, I have everyone here. Can you see us on your screen?" Jack asked.

"Yes. What do you have for me?"

Joe said, "I'll start. The farmhouse was leased to twenty-four-year-old Nassim Nasr and his wife, Sera. She was the woman injured in the shootout. They moved in about three months ago. Two of those months he was working in Kansas on a work assignment as a welder. By the way, Max, I talked to the landlord, a Ms. Shellie Blum, and she is really pissed about all the damage to her property and is threatening to sue Homeland Security for the damages and for the rest of the year-long lease."

"Send me her contact info and I'll take care of it."

Joe continued. "Terrorist number two, Rami Zein, was thirty-five years old. He was a controls engineer and was the suicide bomber in the backyard. He received an electrical engineering degree from Purdue University in 2005. I could not find any work history on Zein, but I'm still working on it. Terrorist number three, Hassan Haddad, was twenty-two years old and the deceased one in the kitchen. Haddad was an independent tanker truck driver who owned his own rig."

Max asked, "What did he haul? Fuel?"

"I'm not sure, but he made several deliveries for Chem Co. Products in El Paso, Texas. Deliveries were in and out of Mexico and parts of the U.S. and Canada."

Max leaned toward the screen. "I really need to know what he was hauling from Chem Co. I'd like you and Doug to go to Chem Co. and find out when and what he was delivering for them."

"We'll book a red-eye flight tonight and be there tomorrow," answered Doug.

"Great, I knew I could depend on you two."

Jack had a question for Joe. "Did you say Haddad owned his own rig? How does a twenty-two-year-old buy a one-hundred-and-fifty-thousand-dollar truck?"

Max interrupted. "I think we need a family history on all our dead terrorists."

"I agree, some things are not adding up," Doug replied, rubbing his chin with his thumb and index finger. Doug began to describe his interview with Sera, the wife. "When I got to the hospital the next day, she was already out of surgery and alert. She had a bowel resection. The surgeon says she was lucky not to have more damaged organs. Sera says she does not know who or what her husband was into or what he was planning. He never talked to her that much, and only about family affairs. He told her it was her duty to never doubt him or ask about his work, and to always devote all her time and energy to taking care of him and their son. And so she did. She asked me if we would put someone in prison for life for being a faithful wife and mother? I told her that her son was in good hands and well taken of. I believed her story. She seemed sincere. The usual dominated Muslim female."

Diane jumped in next. "After going through all the phone contacts, text messages, and emails, we found fifty-nine hits on a college professor named Yassir Kassar. Mr. Kassar was a professor at Wichita University in Kansas. He was a physics professor for twelve years and retired three years ago. He's now living on a small ranch northwest of Wichita." Diane nodded toward Jack. "He seemed harmless at first until Jack dug deeper into his background. He was a key scientist in developing nuclear weapons in Pakistan during the late 1980s. Fearing he could be kidnapped by terrorists for his expertise, he and his family fled Pakistan for the U.S. and applied for political asylum. Max, Jack, and I would like to go to Kansas tomorrow and pay a visit to Mr. Kassar," Diane requested.

"By all means, go and check him out. Perhaps he feels he or his family are in grave danger of a kidnapping? We need some answers and we need them now," stressed Max.

Jack informed Max the Suburbans had been repaired and would be ready to pick up in the morning.

Max concluded the meeting by saying, "I know you all have been working very hard, but there is no letting up. We could be close to finding these terrorists, or we may not even be in the ballpark. It's do-or-die time. America is depending on you all. Not trying to put any added stress on you, but we are inside a pressure cooker and it's beginning to boil! Keep up the good work, and Godspeed!"

After the screen went black from Max's end, Doug turned to the rest in the room. "I need a drink. Come on, Joe! Jack, are you up for it?"

"Nope, my friend. This old man needs to sleep," Jack complained.

Diane added, "I'm exhausted, too. Goodnight, guys."

2:17 a.m.

The phone rang in Jack's room, startling him from a sound sleep. "Hello, what's the problem?"

Diane asked, "Jack, are you awake?"

"I am now, Princess!"

"I'm sorry to wake you, but I can't sleep. I keep replaying in my head, over and over, shooting the suicide bomber. I have one question for you. How did you know he was running toward us to kill us and himself? How did you know he wasn't running to us for help?"

"That's two questions. I'll answer the second one first. No one that wanted to stay alive would leave the cover of a building and run into the line of fire. And how did I know he wanted to kill us? He was wearing a backpack and he was running with his fingers straight out on one hand and the other hand was making a fist. No one runs like that. No one. He was holding the detonator, called a dead man's switch, in his right hand. As soon as he took his thumb off the plunger, it exploded. You had no choice," he assured Diane. "A few more steps and we would be dead right now. Your dad would be attending your funeral today. These terrorists were planning to kill as many Americans as possible. Women and children included. It doesn't matter to them. You saved many lives. Your dad will be so proud of you, Princess. Now go to sleep. You will be driving some tomorrow and I need you to be awake."

"Thank you, Jack. I'll let you go back to sleep," she mumbled.

"Goodnight, Diane, sleep tight."

The next morning, after the four agents met for breakfast, they went to pick up their Suburbans at the repair shop and then said their goodbyes as they left in different directions.

Jack drove the first leg of the way to Wichita.

After a few hours on the road, Diane said, "Sorry I woke you up last night. I've always known shooting someone might be a part of this job, but I've never killed anyone before. I somehow convinced myself I would be interviewing people, working on clues, and doing a lot of data mining. Crunching numbers or something, not be in an actual firefight!"

"Diane, I have been in combat many times. The way you handled yourself this week was as good as any soldier I ever served with. I am lucky to have you as my partner. I have one hundred percent faith that you will do the right thing–whenever and whatever is necessary."

"Thanks, Jack, that means a lot to me."

"You're welcome, Princess. We all must do things in this job we wouldn't dream of doing on our own. Seldom, if ever, do we get a do-over. And regardless of what happens in the end, we must live with ourselves. You have to believe in your cause or agenda, something greater than yourself."

CHAPTER 10

June 28 at 4:00 p.m.
Fort Meade, Maryland

KATIA LOOKED AT her wristwatch, then closed out of her computer programs and turned off her computer. She reached into her desk drawer, picked up a flash drive with the new spying software program, and slipped it into the side pocket of her purse. She turned off the lights as she left her office and locked the door. She walked down the hallway to Karen Waters' office. She poked her head in the doorway. "Thanks again, Karen, for letting me visit my Aunt Nadia. I promise I'll be back in a week."

"I know she means the world to you, Katia. If you require more time, you let me know and I'll give it to you," Karen said with a smile. "Diane told me a little about her, and your mom, and how the three of you escaped Russia."

Katia smiled. "I was only seven years old. Mom, Aunt Nadia, and I walked for eighty straight days across Russia, then sneaked across the border until we made it to Germany at the U.S. Embassy in West Berlin. They took turns carrying me when I was too fatigued to walk. I remember being so very cold and hungry, and strangers letting us sleep in their homes and in their barns. Nadia would tell me not to worry, that God would help us to be free.

"This is why I work here, Karen. Freedom is everything to me. The youth today take it for granted here in America.

I'm afraid they have been deceived, and one day will lose it."

"I share your sentiment. Drive safe, Katia. Tell your Aunt Nadia I'm proud to call her an American, and I will be praying for her."

"Thank you."

"If you meet up with Diane, tell her we're all proud of her and miss her. See you in a week."

Katia had one more stop before heading to Chicago. She drove through Fort Meade's rush hour traffic to Diane's apartment. She unlocked the door, walked in, and turned on a small table lamp. In the kitchen, everything seemed normal. Then she slowly stepped into the bedroom, walked over to the bed, and raised the head end of the mattress. There was Diane's black pistol, just as she said it would be. Slowly picking up the pistol, she gently held the gun flat in both palms.

This must be the graduation gift from her father.

DG was engraved on the handgrip and *Princess Warrior* engraved on the side of the slide. She took the magazine out and pulled back on the slide, ejecting a cartridge out of the gun. She had second thoughts about taking the pistol with her. Her memories flashed back to her childhood. The Russian checkpoints still haunted her. As they crossed by the guards, they always had their guns pointed at her mother and aunt. Her mother would squeeze her hand so tight and she felt her mother tremble with fear until they were allowed to pass. Guns had always scared her, even as an adult.

Chicago has very strict gun laws.

She didn't know the area in Chicago she was visiting. All she heard about Chicago was the gang-related violence and murders on TV news.

She sat on the bed and wondered, *what should I do?*

CHAPTER 11

July 2 at 10:15 a.m.
El Paso International Airport

AGENTS DOUG DICKINSON and Joe Thomas arrived at the airport and rented a white 2018 Suburban. As they left the airport for Chem Co., located a stone's throw away from the Rio Grande river, Doug said, "I don't have a good feeling about this place," as he slipped behind the wheel.

Joe was fastening his seatbelt. "In what way?"

"I don't know. I can't put my finger on it."

"Well, we'll know soon enough if this is a wasted lead."

Forty-five minutes later Doug and Joe met with the company's owner and manager, Cliff Campbell.

"Good morning, I am FBI Special Agent Doug Dickinson, and this is Special Agent Joe Thomas, working in conjunction with the Homeland Security Counterterrorism Division. We are here today to ask you some questions about a delivery tanker driver by the name of Hassan Haddad. But before we start, I want to remind you that lying to an FBI agent is a federal crime. The standard felony punishment is five years in a federal prison. Now then, what was Haddad hauling for you, and to what locations were these shipments delivered?"

"Is the driver in some kind of trouble? He is not an employee, just a contract driver. We have many drivers delivering for us. We've never had a problem with any of them in the past," Cliff insisted.

"We are just doing a routine investigation. Can we see a list of the products, quantities, and customers' locations that were delivered by Mr. Haddad? Or should I call in for a search warrant?" Doug asked with a glare.

"Oh no, no, we want to cooperate. Let's go down and talk to the shipping and receiving manager."

The three of them walked through the huge building, full of large storage tanks and boxes stacked from the floor to the massive ceiling. There were about thirty busy employees filling orders, and forklift trucks carrying skids stacked high roamed about.

"This is some operation you have here, Cliff," Joe stated.

"Thanks, we are the largest distributor of these chemicals in North America. We sell soaps, waxes, fuel additives, and propellants, as well as many other chemicals. We have military contracts with many countries and industrial customers in almost every state."

After a few hours spent pulling files with Ruth Sells, the shipping and receiving manager, the agents had a complete list of Haddad's deliveries.

Joe noticed a security camera and asked Ruth, "Do you keep your security camera videos?"

"Yes, we keep them for a year because of the nature of some products, and at our customers' request."

"It might be helpful if we could see Haddad picking up his loads," Doug added.

"Okay, I'll call Cliff and tell him you are on your way. He can take you to the head of security; he keeps all the videos on the company server's hard drive," Ruth replied.

Doug folded up the list and placed it in his pocket. "Thank you, Ms. Sells. You have been very helpful."

"You're welcome. Good luck with your investigation,

gentlemen."

A few minutes later Cliff led the agents down to the security office, where they studied videos of Haddad and his truck, a white tanker trailer. As they scanned more video, they noticed Haddad also drove a yellow and a blue tanker trailer with the same DOT identification numbers.

Doug asked, "Joe, have any of these other tanker trailers been recovered?"

"None," Joe replied.

"Run these DOT ID numbers through, and let's see what turns up."

Joe called in the numbers to an FBI national databank. A few minutes later he told Doug and Cliff, "These numbers are bogus. They don't exist."

Doug highlighted Haddad's last five deliveries on a handful of packing slips. "Look here, Joe, they were all to a Jayhawk Paint and Coating Inc. located in Kansas. The last delivery was about ten weeks ago."

"Cliff, how long has Jayhawk Paint and Coating been a customer of yours?" Joe asked.

"They are a recent customer, so maybe six months?"

Doug continued to mark the delivery manifests as he spoke. "And would you say they are good customers? Pay on time?"

"Let's go back to my office so I can pull up our invoices," Cliff answered, as a few beads of sweat broke out on his brow.

Back in Cliff's office, Doug and Joe were sitting in chairs across the desk from Cliff. The man was no longer smiling—instead, he was dripping sweat as he pulled all the records of sales to Jayhawk Paint and Coating.

"I'm printing you a copy of everything I have, gentlemen," he said as he walked over to the printer and retrieved them. "Our contact there was a Mr. Bob Johnson. Here is the bank's routing number. He paid the company's invoices on the same day he received them, via electronic banking. The purchases started in February. The first was six thousand gallons of Lox, and a few weeks later four deliveries of eight thousand gallons each of RP-1 kerosene."

Joe directed his question to Cliff. "Can I have the names of companies that sell Lox and RP-1 in the United States?"

"Sure thing, Mr. Thomas." Cliff reached into his desk drawer and pulled out a list of names and phone numbers. "Here is a complete list of our competitors. We sometimes buy from them if we don't have enough of something in stock. You know, whatever it takes to fill the order," Cliff replied, nervously dabbing the sweat from his forehead.

"Cliff, would you mind if we used your office to call your competitors?"

Cliff replied after a short pause, "Go right ahead. Make yourselves at home."

"Great. Oh, can I have your fax number too?" Doug asked.

CHAPTER 12

June 29 at 9:45 a.m.
Chicago, Illinois

KATIA PARKED DIANE'S Mustang in the nursing home parking lot and put the windows and top up.

She checked her hair in the rearview mirror. Her cheeks were flushed from the wind. *What a fun car to drive.*

It worked to keep her thoughts about her feelings about her Aunt Nadia's grave condition away. Katia put on her brave and happy face before leaving the car.

The Lakeshore Nursing home was an upscale facility. It was a newer single-story brick building with large windows that ran down the entire length. She walked through the double glass doors into a lobby with a sitting area off to the side and a hallway leading to a large half-circle desk at the nurse's station.

A pretty blonde in a nurse's uniform greeted her.

"Hi, my name is Katia and I'm here to see my aunt, Nadia Ivanov."

"I'm Nancy Mushinski, nursing supervisor of the day shift. Pleased to meet you. Nadia has been telling us for a week, and about ten times a day, you were coming to see her." She waved toward a chair in an alcove. "Let's have a seat. I'd like to speak with you before you see her."

Katia sat down in one of the wing-backed chairs, across from the nurse.

"Katia, I'm so sorry to tell you this, but Nadia is at the end-of-life stage and losing her battle with cancer. She wants to see you before she dies. I want to assure you that her pain medicine is working well, and she is almost pain-free. She is a sweetheart and a very strong-willed woman." Nancy leaned over and placed her hand on Katia's. "She is a favorite of all the nurses and staff here. If you need anything, anything at all, you come and see me. Your aunt is in room one-eleven, down this hall and on the left."

A tear trickled down Katia's cheek. "Thank you. Did you say one-eleven? Her birthday is January eleventh."

Nancy nodded and squeezed her shoulder as she stood and went back to her post at the front desk.

Katia rose and walked down the long hall as she wiped her tears from her eyes. She took a deep breath before she entered Nadia's room. Nadia was lying on her side, staring out the window.

A bright red hummingbird feeder hung from a small maple tree as green hummingbirds darted around it.

"Nadia, I'm finally here!"

She rolled over and a large smile appeared on her pale face. She looked much older than Katia's memory of her.

She bent down and gave Nadia a long hug. "I love you, Nadia. I always will, forever, here on Earth and in heaven."

Tears ran down both their cheeks.

"Katia, I am so proud of you! To think a Russian girl is serving to protect our great new country, America!"

"It does seem kind of funny," she replied in Russian.

"Dear, you see the box on top of my dresser? Take it with you when you leave, but do not open it until I'm in heaven. Can you do this?"

"Of course!"

"It's important that you wait until I die first before you see the contents."

"Should I be worried, Aunt Nadia?"

"No, no, dear. It's a surprise!"

"Okay, I'll take it now and lock it up in the trunk of the car."

"One more thing I want to request, my dear."

"You know I'll do anything you want, what is it?"

"I want you to take my ashes to Ellis Island, at the base of the Statute of Liberty, and release them as a symbol of my freedom. Can you do this for me, sweetheart?"

"I would be honored to. I would have no freedom myself if it was not for you and your Mother. I love that you picked there as your final resting place, Aunt Nadia." She gave her aunt another long hug and told her she would always love her.

Nurse Nancy placed a bed for Katia in Nadia's room. They laughed and cried, cherishing every moment together. The nurses who'd become friends with Nadia would stop in and visit her. Katia remained in the room with her aunt until she passed on a few days later.

Katia bought all the nurses gift cards for being so nice to Nadia and herself. She handed them out as she said her goodbyes to the staff. Now she was on to the task of finding Diane. She needed the comforting words of a good friend.

CHAPTER 13

July 2

DIANE'S CELL PHONE rang. "Hi, Katia, I missed you! How is your Aunt Nadia? She did… I'm so sorry to hear that. I'm glad you had the opportunity to spend some time with her… You are an awesome niece, Katia… Nope, Jack and I are no longer in Dearborn, we are heading to Wichita, Kansas. How far is Wichita to Chicago?… Let me see…" Diane opened her laptop. "It's about seven hundred miles, or about an eleven or twelve-hour drive, depending on traffic."

"Diane, does Katia still want to meet up and give us the latest hacking software?"

Diane put her hand over the phone. "She does, Jack, but I'm trying to talk her out of it. It's too dangerous. I don't want to see her get hurt," Diane said in a quiet voice.

Jack agreed with her. They didn't need to get any non-combatants in the line of fire. "Tell her we have gotten along so far without it. I think we'll get by okay."

"Jack and I think you need to go back home. We'll be fine without it. Be safe and God bless you, dear."

"Okay, I'll call as soon as I get back to Fort Meade."

"Bye, my friend. I'll see you soon."

Diane put her cell back in her pocket. "I feel bad for Katia, her aunt died in her arms. I could tell her heart is breaking."

Jack noticed her eyes tearing up. "That's too bad, but I would think dying in the arms of a loved one is the best way to die. I think maybe heaven is just a little sweeter."

"Oh, I wish had thought of that when I was talking to her."

"Why don't you text it to her?"

"Good idea. Thanks, I will."

After a few more hours behind the wheel, Jack pulled over to the shoulder of the road and stopped. "Would you like to drive a while, Princess? I need to make some calls."

"Sure." Diane slid out the door and walked around the Suburban. She did some stretches and ended up leaning on the hood of the car, doing a few leg lifts.

Jack found this slightly amusing. "We're not going to race each other, are we?"

Diane laughed. "Why? Are you afraid I'd kick your ass?"

"You know it," Jack replied.

"Do we even know where we are going when we get there?"

They both climbed back in the SUV and she pulled out on the highway.

"Not yet, not until I make these calls. Just keep heading toward Wichita."

A few minutes later, Jack called the university. "This is Jack Jacobs of Homeland Security Counterterrorism Division. I'm calling regarding professor Yassir Kassar."

"Professor Kassar no longer teaches at the university," the secretary replied.

"Is there someone still there who might be in contact with, or know of, Professor Kassar that I might speak to?"

"I'm not sure I can divulge that information over the phone," the secretary replied.

"I understand; I'm going to email my director's phone

number right now to the university. You can look up the Director of Counterterrorism at Homeland Security and verify the number. And if this is not sufficient proof then I guess I'll have to call in for a warrant and secure all documents concerning the professor and the university. Including all students' names since he was first employed there. I just have a few questions. I'll hold while you decide which way you want me to proceed."

"One moment, Mr. Jacobs," she replied in an annoyed tone.

Jack glanced at Diane. "When you have to pressure someone… not being rude usually pays dividends."

Twenty seconds later: "Clayton Pluckebaum was an associate professor under Professor Kassar. I can give you his number?"

"That would be helpful. Thank you very much."

A few minutes later after he received Clayton's number. "While I have him on the speakerphone, do you think we should record a voiceprint of him?"

"Why not, it will never be any easier." She reached for her laptop.

Jack immediately called the professor. "Professor Pluckebaum?"

"Yes."

"This is Special Agent Jack Jacobs of Homeland Security Counterterrorism Division. I'm calling in reference to a friend and coworker of yours, a Professor Kassar."

"Has something happened to him? Is he in some kind of trouble?" Professor Pluckebaum asked.

He looked over to Diane and nodded his head to her.

"Just a routine background check," Jack reassured him. "Someone suggested he might become a target for a possible kidnapping because of his background involvement with nuclear weapons, so we are doing threat assessments on all persons with similar backgrounds as Professor Kassar. What can you tell me about him?" Jack inquired.

"He was very passionate about teaching physics to his students," Professor Pluckebaum replied.

"Well, why did he quit teaching, if he was so passionate?"

"I'm not sure why he left the university, Mr. Jacobs. He just came into the classroom one day and said, 'I'm done.' He didn't seem upset or anything, so it's still kind of a mystery to me."

"What did the university say to explain his quitting to the students?"

"Basically, they just said he was retiring."

"Clayton–can I call you Clayton?"

"Sure."

"So, Clayton, do you still see Kassar or meet with him? You know… socially?"

"Yes, he still comes to the university occasionally to do research on one of his projects."

Diane whispered, "What kind?"

"What kind of projects would a retired professor work on?" Jack asked.

"He was consistently conducting experiments of some kind. You know, you can take a man out of the physics department, but you can't take the physics department out of the man."

They both laughed.

"So, I take it he still lives close by?"

"Yes, he bought a small ranch about fifteen miles northwest of Wichita."

"Did he? Does he have a family here?"

"Yes, he has a wife, and his children are grown."

"Has he ever said anything or seemed concerned for his personal safety?"

"No, not that I know of."

"Was he active outside the classroom with students?"

"Well, he did mentor students of the Muslim faith on occasion."

"Would you consider him an activist when it comes to his faith?"

"I'm not sure what you mean by 'activist'?"

"Did he promote Sharia law?"

"I don't have any idea. Maybe, but I can't speak for him, so you'll have to ask him yourself."

"Did he ever seem upset with American values?"

Diane whispered to him, "Compton?" and threw her hands palms up.

"You'll have to ask him yourself."

"Okay, one last question, Clayton, did he ever mention Compton?"

"You mean Arthur Compton? Arthur was a major influence on him in the understanding of physics. He quoted him all the time."

Diane said, "There's your connection."

"Has he ever said anything that raised a red flag or concern for you?"

"Kassar asked me a question once that has haunted me ever since. He asked me, if I had the power to stop the world from destroying itself, would I use it? I said, in a heartbeat. He said, 'I bet you would, I bet you would.' And then he just walked away."

Jack glanced over to Diane and nodded his head. "Well, thank you, Clayton, for cooperating with me. I must ask you to keep this conversation to yourself for national security reasons. I may be in contact with you again soon. Have a great day and a great Fourth of July. Goodbye."

"I think we might be on to something, Diane."

"Sure does sound like it," she replied, tapping her fingers on the sides of the steering wheel.

"Time will tell, but we have to be ready for anything. Hey, I just remembered I have a friend who lives somewhere around here. I think I'll give him a call to see if maybe he has heard of Professor Kassar."

"Who is that?"

"Chris Finley, we spent a little time in Iraq together. He's a good man. He got out of the service and started his own trucking company here in Kansas. I always told him if I ever got to Kansas, I'd look him up. Well, here I am.

"Chris, how you doing? Jack Jacobs. Hey, my friend, guess what? I'm in Kansas on my way to Wichita. Give me a call when you hear this." Jack ended the call and reached behind the seat to retrieve his laptop. "I thought I would look at some satellite pictures of the professor's ranch, so we can case the area before we get there. Do you know any better sites than Google Earth on the web, Diane?"

"Yes, I do, but you will want several pictures from different dates if you are looking for changes to his property. One picture won't give you any comparison. Hand me my phone."

He handed her the phone.

"Good, I have four bars on my phone. Can you hear me now?"

They both chuckled.

"I'm calling my boss at the office… I'll put it on speaker." She placed the phone in the holder on the dash and put in her Bluetooth. "Hi… Karen Waters, please… Thank you. Karen, it's Diane. How is everything going back at the office?"

"We're good, Diane. How is the investigation going? Are you teaching those Homeland Security boys some new tricks?"

"Karen, you know what they say about teaching old dogs new tricks," Diane answered. She looked at Jack and said quietly, "Just kidding, Jack.

"My partner, Jack Jacobs, is requesting time-lapse photos fifteen miles northwest of Wichita. Can we get that through the National Reconnaissance Office? Tell the NRO it involves the highest priority Blackbird investigation, and they can call Max Braude at Homeland. He is the head of the CT division."

"Okay, Diane, I'll give it a whirl. Can you email me an address and zip code?"

"You'll have it in two minutes."

"Okay, great. Oh, another thing, Diane. I got a call from Katia. She was almost back to Fort Meade when she felt bad and stopped at a motel to rest a bit. She said she was overcome by a feeling to go to Kansas. She says it felt like a message from God."

"I told her this mission could be dangerous, and I didn't want to see her get hurt!"

"I called HR, and she has another two weeks of vacation available. I can't tell her what she can or can't do on her own time."

"Okay, we will keep an eye out for her. Thanks, KJ, you are a lifesaver!"

"You're more than welcome. Please be safe and take care. Bye."

"I'll be back in my chair before you know it, KJ."

Diane gave Jack the email address of Karen J. Waters and the location of Professor Kassar's ranch so she could send him the satellite photos.

* * *

6:45 p.m.

Katia was rolling down the Interstate, heading away from the sun, on her way back home to Fort Meade. She was exhausted from driving and having trouble keeping her eyes open. Seeing a Tin Roof Motel off the next exit, she decided to call it a day and get some much-needed sleep.

She parked Diane's car and put the top up while she reached under the seat for Diane's SIG Sauer P226 pistol and tucked it into the side pocket of her laptop case. She grabbed a carry-on bag and the unopened box she received from her Aunt Nadia.

After checking in and finding her room, she set her bags down next to the bed and collapsed. She was anxious to know what was in the box Aunt Nadia left her. She opened it slowly and found some newspaper articles about their escape by walking a thousand miles across Communist Russia. There were many photographs of her mother and Aunt Nadia, as well as many old pictures of Katia.

Underneath the old pictures was a white envelope with 'Dear Katia' written on it, and under that, there was a big yellow envelope. She opened the white one first and found a letter.

My Dearest Katia,

I thought, now that I'm in heaven, you should know the truth. When I was fifteen years old, I met this boy, I got into trouble. By that, I mean pregnant. In those days, it meant I would be labeled a whore and would have to have an abortion. My sister—your mother—and I ran away from home. She took care of me and the baby. She worked night and day to feed us. We told everyone the baby was hers and her husband died in a work-related accident. She devoted her life to you. Yes, I am your birth mother. We both raised you and loved you equally. After we escaped Russia and came to America, we kind of drifted apart. We decided to keep on living the lie to keep you from being hurt. We both knew you were special to God.

I paid most of your college expenses, as I could save more than your mother over the years. I got a better job and saved most of my income for you. Your fight for liberty and freedom began before you were born, so I took it as a sign from God when you went to work for the NSA. I am so proud of the woman you have grown into. I will watch over you here in heaven until you join us.

Love forever,
Nadia

Tears flowed down her cheeks as she realized why there was a special, strong bond between her and Aunt Nadia. Two mothers loved her. Katia felt so loved, and at the same time so lonely. Both had gone to heaven.

And what did Nadia mean, she saw my job at the NSA as a sign from God?

Physically tired and now emotionally drained, she peeked into the big yellow envelope. Inside were a bunch of loose hundred-dollar bills. She spread them out on the bedspread, counted the money, and stacked them in one thousand-dollar piles on the bed. Ten thousand dollars in cash lay before her, and a little note that read:

Dear Katia,

After my estate is settled you will collect what is left.

Love,
Your other mother, Nadia

I want to make Nadia proud of me. I must go to Kansas and find Diane. I must do my part.

She closed her eyes and drifted off to sleep thinking of Diane and what she would tell her of her dear Aunt Nadia.

* * *

July 2

After receiving a briefing from Doug Dickinson, Max called Jack. "Hey, Jack, Max here. How far are you from Topeka?"

"Couple hours away, I think. What's up?"

"Your terrorist friend, the tanker truck driver, delivered thirty-two thousand gallons of Kerosene RP-1 and six gallons of Lox to a Jayhawk Paint and Coating Corporation in Topeka. I would like for you and Diane to investigate the business and see if they know our driver."

"No problem, Max, it happens to be right on our way."

"Doug and Joe are en route back to Dearborn to follow up on a person of interest, and after that, I will probably send them to you for backup."

Jack said, "I think we are making progress. I talked to an

associate professor to Professor Kassar. He said Arthur Crompton had a profound impact on him, so I think Professor Kassar is our tie-in with Compton. I just don't know if he is a terrorist or a future victim of one. But I will find out one way or the other. You can count on us."

"I *am* counting on you, Jack. Overseas chatter about Blackbird has ramped up over the last forty-eight hours. Whatever Blackbird is, it will occur soon. We have the Coast Guard on both coasts and our US Border Patrol in the South on high alert. Report back on what you learn in Topeka. Godspeed, my friend."

Jack looked at Diane. "Put the pedal to the metal, Princess."

"Did Max say the tanker driver was hauling Kerosene RP-1 and Lox? Do you know what you have when you mix those together?"

"No, I was a history major. I hated chemistry!"

"Well, Captain Jack, I got straight A's in chemistry. You mix those and you have rocket fuel. Kerosene RP-1 is a highly flammable refined kerosene."

"Well, Miss 'Straight A' Princess, could the Kerosene RP-1 be used as a paint thinner additive?"

"It could, but it would be very costly. Kerosene RP-1 is not a cheap product. It is highly refined, which makes it sound suspicious to me."

"I think we're an hour away from finding out," Jack answered.

* * *

THE BLACKBIRD THREAT

Fort Bragg, North Carolina

"Max, Colonel Glass here."

"Yes, Colonel, what can I help you with?"

"I just called to see how Diane was working out for you. I haven't heard from her. I've been back in Iraq for a couple days."

"Jim, I'm not sure if I should tell you or if you should hear it from Diane."

"What the hell is going on, Max?" the colonel asked with an angry tone.

"It's all good, Colonel. Diane and her partner, Jack Jacobs, were en route to Dearborn and came to the aid of another team working in the Dearborn area when the other team stumbled into an ambush. It just so happened Diane and Jack were just minutes away, so they went in as backup. Diane took out two of the three terrorists. We here are very proud of the work she is doing, Jim."

"I didn't know her assignment would involve an active response to a combat scenario."

"We really don't know what will happen to these teams working the Blackbird threat, because they are the point of the spear, so to speak. They must be ready for anything and everything. That's why I paired her up with Jack Jacobs. He is the most experienced of all the personnel I have available working this case. I have a hundred percent trust in Jack." Max hesitated. How much information should he give one of his agent's fathers, even if he was a colonel? "Right now, it appears something may happen in Kansas, but we don't have enough intel yet."

"I think it might be a good idea if I dispatch a couple of Special Response Teams to Fort Riley, just in case some backup is needed. If you don't mind, Max."

"After what happened in Dearborn, I must agree with you, Jim. My agents are spread thin with all the leads they are working. I'll put in a request to JSOC and General Martin for the teams."

"Great, I'll put the operational orders together and have two teams in Fort Riley in the morning. Max, let me know if you need other teams in other locations."

"Will do, Colonel. I'll let Jack and Diane know they will have backup if needed."

"Let me know if anything changes, Max."

"Will do, Colonel."

It didn't take the colonel long to contact Fort Riley. "First Sergeant, get me the base commander at Fort Riley on the phone, reserve two Black Hawks, and inform Delta Force SRTs Blue and Silver of a new mission. Have them gather all their gear, we leave at zero six hundred. Also, notify TF160 I'll need two birds for the mission exercise."

"Yes sir!"

***

Diane slowed down driving in the heavy Topeka traffic. "Am I even on the right street?"

"You are, just stay straight and hang a right on Castleway Drive. Jayhawks Paint and Coating should be just ahead on your side of the street. There's our street." Jack pointed. "It's clear. You can get over into the turn lane."

"Okay, Captain."

"Just a couple of weeks ago, did you ever think you would be driving around in Topeka, Kansas?" Jack asked with a grin.

"I'm not sure how you do it, Jack. Not knowing where you are going from one minute to the next. Not having any routine at all, twenty-four hours a day," she said, shaking her head. "The problem with routines is they work against you in the spying business. Being predictable can get you killed. Being unpredictable gives you a tactical advantage."

"According to Google Maps, that large blue building is Jayhawks Paint and Coatings."

"I see their sign." Diane pulled into an empty parking lot. Tall weeds were growing in the cracks in the pavement and scattered broken glass littered the parking lot.

"Looks like no one is home or has been for a while. Certainly no one to talk to. I'll go across the street to that service station. I'll ask someone if they know anything about this company."

"Roger that." Diane stayed behind in the SUV.

Jack entered the gas station and flashed his Homeland Security badge. He asked for the manager or owner.

A heavy-set man sitting behind the old gray metal counter responded, "That would be me."

"Hi, what can you tell me about the business across the street? When did Jayhawks Paint go out of business?"

The manager scratched his stubbly chin. "About three years ago. They were my biggest customer. Really took a chunk of change out of my pocket. I sold their employees thousands of gallons of gas each month. It broke my heart when they closed. I came damn close to going out of business too."

"Have you seen any activity in their building in the last three years? Anyone lease any space?"

"Can't say I've seen anybody, except investors and real estate people touring the space."

"Okay, thanks for the info. You have a nice day."

"You too."

Diane was standing outside the Suburban, stretching her legs. "What's the word, Jack?"

"It's a no-go here. Unfortunately, we're chasing ghosts. Jayhawks Paint went out of business three years ago. I'll call Max and let him know.

"Max, this is Jack. Hey, Jayhawks Paint and Coating went out of business three years ago. Can you email me the invoices and payment receipts, including the bank routing numbers, for the Kerosene RP-1?"

"Why the routing info, Jack?"

"It's better if you don't ask, Max."

"Okay, you got it. Be careful. Don't make me sorry. Understand?"

"Roger that, Max. Talk to you soon."

Jack circled around to the driver's side. "Hey, do you care if I drive a while? I have a mission for you."

"Don't tell me you want to hack into some bank. Who do you think I am? You need a FISA warrant for that, or to go through the IRS."

"No time for that, and I'm not building a case for court. Have you ever heard the saying, 'No blood, no foul'?"

"I could get into trouble for hacking into banks, Jack."

"I'm not telling," he said with a grin. "We're just following the money, not taking it."

"Okay, just this once, but I'm not liking it."

"Duly noted. Hack away, Princess Warrior. Hack away."

One hour later, Diane came up for air. "Okay, here's what I found out. An account was opened at the First Bank of Topeka six and a half months ago. Money was deposited by a wire transfer from an offshore bank in the Bahamas. The person to contact was a man named Robert Johnson. The money deposited in the Bahamas by wire transfer came from a bank in Yemen. And the trail stops there. I'm surprised no one picked up on these transactions."

Jack's ringtone sounded. "Hi, Chris, I see you got my message… How are you doing? … We are rolling down I-35, about a half an hour away from Wichita. How close are you to there?… That is pretty close… I don't know. We haven't reserved any rooms yet. I appreciate the offer, but I don't want to put you out or anything… Let me ask my partner." Jack turned in his seat a bit toward Diane. "Chris wants to know if we want to stay at his ranch while we are in town. He says he has two empty bedrooms."

"I guess so. I could whip up a home-cooked meal for you guys if you'd like. I was taught by the best cooks in the officers' mess hall."

"She says it will be fine… Okay, my friend, give me your address and I'll feed it to my phone. See you in about forty-five minutes.

"Thanks for doing this. You're going to like Chris. He's a real stand-up guy."

"To tell you the truth, between living out of this Suburban and motel rooms I'm starting to have claustrophobia."

They both laughed.

"I bet Chris's ranch will feel like a castle," she said with a sigh.

"We'll know soon."

A few minutes later Diane informed Jack, "We're almost there, according to the GPS. I'm surprised this works so well even on gravel roads."

"One of the best apps ever created for a phone. Especially if you are a spy," Jack said with a smile, and Diane returned it with a beaming smile of her own.

"I bet that smile gets you out of a lot of trouble."

"Yes, it does. It's my secret weapon and, if necessary, karate is my backup."

They both laughed.

"No, it's true," she joked.

"Hey, this must be his house on the left. It's the only one around." Jack pulled into the driveway of a nice older two-story brick home with a three-car attached garage. A small stream of smoke was wafting from behind the house. A brown and black German Shepherd jumped off a wrap-around porch and made a beeline for the Suburban.

"That's Sadie. I recognize her from his social media accounts." He hopped out of the Suburban and yelled, "Come here, Sadie!"

Sadie barked and ran right to Jack as he kneeled down, posing no threat to Sadie. She wagged her tail back at Jack.

"Come on out and play, Diane. She won't hurt you." Jack slowly rubbed Sadie's belly.

Diane slowly eased out of the Suburban. "So now you're a dog whisperer?"

A muscular man with short blond hair walked around the corner of the house. "I heard Sadie using her *I spotted a weasel* bark. How the hell are you, Jack? I thought I would never see you again!" Chris extended his hand as he approached.

Jack took it in a firm grasp and pulled him in over Sadie's wiggling body. "You never know when, or where, a weasel will pop up."

After a quick man-hug, they both turned to face Diane.

"Chris, this is my partner, Diane."

The two exchanged handshakes.

"Glad to meet you, Diane."

"Jack has nothing but praise for you, Chris," replied Diane.

Chris smiled and glanced at Jack. "I hope you two are hungry. I have some porterhouse steaks to put on the grill."

"Sounds awesome, my friend," Jack said as the three of them walked to the back of the house, with Sadie wagging her tail right beside them.

"So, Diane, how long have you been working for Homeland Security?" Chris asked.

"I don't work for them. I'm on loan just for this mission."

"She works for the NSA. She's a cyber warrior in the top-secret Tailored Access Ope- rations," Jack informed Chris.

"Jack, can I have a word with you in private?"

"Sure, Diane," he replied.

"I'm going to get the steaks out of the freezer, be right back," Chis mumbled, stepping back through the back door, leaving the two to talk.

"Okay, Jack, two things," she said, anger showing on her red face. "One, how did you know I work in the TAO? I never told you! Two, why in the hell did you tell Chris about my department? That is classified higher than Top Secret. It's Controlled Access. I could lose my security clearance if anyone learns about what I do."

"Relax, Diane, I just guessed you worked in the TAO from all the hacking equipment you know how to operate. And Chris? Well, I trust him with my life. He is nice enough to let us stay here for as long as it takes. I have been in combat with this man. You have my word no one will ever know. Your secret is safe with us."

"Okay, this time, but don't ever speak of me and the TAO together in the same breath. Better yet, never mention the TAO again. Or someone may find our bones out in a desert somewhere."

"I don't take threats very well, Diane."

"I said *our* bones, Jack. I'm saying I would be the first one to go. Since we have had a few whistleblowers in the past, everyone is always under suspicion, even though we have sworn an oath of secrecy at all costs."

"So, when I asked you to hack into that bank and you acted like that was something you didn't want to do?"

Diane rolled her eyes. "I was acting, okay? I hack shit like banks and foreign governments every day. I just didn't want you to know the extent of what I can hack."

"In case you didn't know, we are on the same team. We may need all your skills if we are to achieve our mission or just survive. Many times, I have done things I'm not too proud of, but to save lives it may be necessary to bend a few rules."

"Okay... I get it. It is very difficult for me to discuss these programs outside of my department. You can understand that, right?"

"Once you become part of the deep state, the only way out is death. That is the reason for the safe room in my home. I know more than they tell the presidents. I've done some very, *very* bad things."

"Is that why you quit the CIA?"

"You don't really quit the CIA. You just become an inactive operative. I didn't want to help the New World Order."

"Oh, my God, Jack, you sound like you're one of the *Men in Black*," she said, laughing.

"Been there, done that," he replied with a wink.

"Now I know you're pulling my leg."

"Am I?" Jack just smiled in return.

"Oh, I forgot to tell you, I got an email from my dad. The

colonel is coming and bringing two Delta Force SRT teams with birds to Fort Riley for a few days, just in case we need some backup. Arriving tomorrow morning."

"Sounds like Max told him about our gun battle in Dearborn." Jack shrugged. "Just guessing by his response. I feel sorry for anyone who causes any harm to you." He grinned wickedly.

Chris stepped through the open patio door carrying a large plate with three one-inch-thick porterhouse steaks hanging over the edges. "I just happen to have three twenty-four-ounce porterhouse steaks of the best grass-fed beef in the country," Chris said with a big smile. "How do you want yours cooked?"

"I'll take mine medium well," Jack replied.

"I want mine medium rare," Diane added.

"Jack said you were a little on the bloodthirsty side," Chris laughed.

Diane rolled her eyes and just nodded her head *yes*.

Chris put the steaks on the hot grill. The sound of sizzling and a wonderful aroma filled the air around the patio. Both Diane and Jack were sitting on a patio swing with their feet up on a small table, their open laptops across their thighs. Chris gave Diane a glass of wine and Jack a large glass of sweet tea.

Diane looked up from her laptop and noticed Chris was ogling her legs and short shorts. "You know, that black Suburban gets pretty warm rolling down the road in the sunlight. Jack doesn't believe in air conditioning. Maybe I should change into something more proper?"

"I'm sorry, Diane," Chris said. "Sadie and I are not used to having such a pretty lady visiting us."

"Thank you, Chris." Diane looked away quickly to avoid

making eye contact.

"Hey, Chris, I bet you met Diane's dad in Iraq."

"Really? He was in the military?"

"Still is," Jack answered. "Remember Spec-cial Ops Delta Commander Ranger Colonel 'Bulletproof' Glass?"

"Are you kidding me?"

"Nope," Jack replied. "Met his daughter, and she is a true daddy's girl. Ninth degree black belt with sniper skills and a world-class computer geek and hacker."

Diane looked at Jack and shook her head. "I'm surprised he remembers my name, Chris. He has been having some short-term memory issues lately."

Jack realized he was in trouble with her again and quickly changed the subject. "I thought you were married, Chris?"

"I was, but not for long. Marcee and I are separated and going through a divorce."

"Sorry to hear," Jack mumbled.

"She said I work too many hours and I care more about the damn business than I do her."

"Well, I guess the business is good, then," Jack said, trying to lighten the mood.

"Business is really good. I have a state contract hauling stone for road and bridge construction all over Kansas. I just purchased a tri-axle dump truck. I can now haul twenty-four tons of stone at a time."

Diane closed her laptop. The steaks were beginning to smell done. "What kind of hours do you work when you are working with the state?"

"Sun-up to sun-down, usually six days a week."

"I can see why your marriage is in trouble." Diane took a sip of wine. "Jack, you should have the satellite images by now. Check and see if you do. If you don't, I'll call my boss and find out why."

"Okay, I'm checking. Yep, there they are." Jack zoomed in and out on the satellite images. "I'm not all that sure of what I'm looking at. I can see the primary residence, and it looks like a few storage buildings and some circles."

"Let me look."

Jack handed her his laptop and almost spilled his glass of sweet tea.

After studying the images, she said, "This photo is when the sun is setting. You can see shadows from the house, barns, or storage buildings. But the circles have no shadows; this indicates they're ground level, or below ground level."

"Hey, Chris, does this area look familiar to you?" Jack retrieved his laptop from Diane.

"Zoom out and see if I can find my place. There's my place right here." Chris pointed toward the bottom of the photo. "See the water tower straight behind my house? It's about a mile away. The ranch you're looking at is about five miles from here as the crow flies. I used to plow some fields near that area when I was a teenager. I think this spot used to be some kind of training center the Air Force had years ago. I don't remember too much about it. I was just a kid, maybe fifteen."

Jack scanned over some newest images. "Well, well, what do we have here? Do you know anybody who has a tanker trailer, Chris?"

"Not around here," he replied.

"Look at this picture. See the tanker trailer parked in front of the barn? What are the odds of a tanker next door to the professor?" Jack asked, leaning toward Diane.

She stood up and leaned over to see what he was looking at. "It could be nothing."

"I think tomorrow we will pay a visit to this barn. I am curious what lurks inside."

"A killer cow, perhaps," Diane said, mocking Jack.

"You never know, Princess, you never know."

"Chris, those steaks are smelling really good," Diane said as she advanced on the barbeque.

Chris poked a fork into a steak. "Diane, does yours look bloody enough?"

"Oh yes, perfect, thank you."

"So, Jack, what's the big deal about a tanker trailer, anyway?" Chris asked as he pushed Diane's steak to the back of the grill, away from the heat.

Jack glanced at Chris. "What I tell you stays here, okay?"

"Sure, Jack, you know you can trust me."

"I know, but this is big, my friend… We stumbled across a person of interest who was recently delivering four eight-thousand-gallon shipments of Kerosene RP-1 to a place in Topeka. Except the business closed three years ago."

"Did you talk to the driver, Jack?" Chris asked.

"Well, I never had the chance. Diane had to put him down."

Chris looked at Diane. *Well, she is the colonel's daughter, all right.* "You said he delivered eight thousand gallons at each delivery? That's kind of strange. All the tanker trailers I've seen hold nine thousand two hundred gallons of fuel."

"Maybe where they were delivered, they only had eight-thousand-gallon storage tanks," Diane countered.

"The reason is that nine thousand two hundred gallons is the maximum weight allowed on the interstates. Fuel averages around eight pounds per gallon. That's nine thousand six hundred pounds under the limit. Just seems strange. Hey, I guess you can make a mighty big boom with thirty-two thousand gallons of kerosene."

"Or make a hell of a flamethrower," Jack joked. He gave Chris a serious look. "Again, Chris, this stays here. Another person of interest is a retired college physics professor who lives on the ranch here in these images. He was a key scientist in the development of the nuclear bomb for Pakistan in the 1990s. We're not sure if he is a potential kidnap victim, maybe he has a new type of weapon, or is a mastermind to a terrorist plot about to happen."

"You know me, Jack, anything you need, you got it. I've put my life on the line many times for our country. I'm proud to know we still have patriots like you and Diane still in the good fight against these bastards."

Chris pulled the steaks off the grill and onto plates.

Jack closed his laptop and stood up to take his plate. "Diane and I are grateful for your hospitality, Chris, letting us stay here, sharing your food and wi-fi. You're the best, my friend."

"I agree." Diane gave Chris a one-armed hug and a kiss on the cheek as she took her plate.

"You're both very welcome. Sadie and I love having your company." Just as if on cue, Sadie started licking Diane's hand.

It was a perfect night. The stars were out in force, competing with the fireflies to light up the night sky. The fire pit flames gave off a warm glow and the crackling sounds of the burning logs competed with the calls of the nocturnal critters.

Chris had a puzzled look on his face. "Jack, why would terrorists strike in Kansas? I mean, we're not much of a target-rich state."

"I don't know, the only thing I can do is agree with you. There are few counter-terrorist assets here. They're mostly on the east and west coasts or large Midwest cities like Chicago or Saint Louis. They would, however, be free to move around us with few eyes watching."

"I guess you're right. We may be a little more trusting out here than other places," Chris added.

Jack and Diane nodded their heads in agreement.

"Jack, do you need my help bringing our gear into the house? I don't think it's a good idea to leave it in the Suburban, even way out here."

"I agree. You just beat me to it."

Chris unfolded out of his chair. "I'll show you to your rooms and help you too." As they began to unload the Suburban, Chris turned to Jack. "Damn, you guys fighting World War Three all by yourselves?"

Jack chuckled. "Better to have it and not need it than to need it and not have it!"

After carrying all the equipment into Chris's home, Diane sat up her cell phone monitoring system and tapped into the cell tower nearest the professor's ranch. The equipment would record and forward his calls to Diane's TAO section to be analyzed.

"All set, now it's time for some shuteye for me," Diane confessed with a yawn.

"You're going to stay in my daughter, Julie's, room. The upstairs room, second on the left. I didn't think Jack would like the pink walls as much as you."

"Thanks, Chris. It sounds perfect. Goodnight, gents."

"Goodnight, Diane, sweet dreams," Chris replied. "You sure you don't want a beer, Jack?"

"No, I'm good, my friend. I'm glad we had the time to catch up and talk about the good old days. I'm really sorry things aren't working out with Marcee. If you want, I'd be happy to talk to her."

"I doubt there is anything you can say at this point, but I appreciate the offer."

"Well, I don't have a stellar past when it comes to relationships, but I can tell you from my own hindsight that I should have fought harder to keep my marriage. I lost a wife, a daughter, and a grandson. And no amount of money can replace family."

They ended up talking for the next two hours before turning in for the night.

CHAPTER 14

July 3 at 5:45 a.m.
Wichita, Kansas

DIANE WOKE UP and while lying in bed, said a little prayer asking God to protect her and Jack. She scanned the room. She had been so tired the night before that she hadn't checked out Julie's belongings. There were sports trophies, school pictures, and a family picture. A sense of sadness overtook her. She remembered the loss of her mother and living with only one parent. She hopped out of bed and shook off her negative feelings. It was time for coffee.

She was the first one up. She located the coffee pot, found the coffee in a cupboard, and got it brewing. She raided the fridge and began frying bacon. As the aroma of bacon filled the house, it awoke Jack and Chris. Like magic, Chris was the first to arrive, followed closely by Jack.

"Have a seat, gents. I hope scrambled eggs are okay; breakfast is served." She set the table with their plates and cups, then set a pot of coffee down in front of them. Laughing, she said, "Well, did you two have a little bromance after I went to bed?"

"You are pure evil, Diane, very cute, but evil. It is good to see Jack hasn't changed a bit except for the extra weight, less hair, and that gray stuff on his head," Chris joked.

Jack looked at Chris and then Diane. "I need more coffee

before I have any comebacks for you two, but it is nice to see you both in a good mood."

"Diane, next time you talk to him, tell your dad I said hi. He saved so many lives. He was like the General Patton of Iraq. Running Special Ops twenty-four seven and keeping the enemy off balance. He made it really hard for them to mount any kind of offensive threat against us," Chris said.

"I know. Dad's not shy about talking about all the war stories over there," she said softly, smiling and nodding her head.

After they finished breakfast, Chris called Sadie over and set his plate on the floor for her to lick it clean. After a few licks, the plate looked spotless. He reached down, picked up the plate, and rubbed the bottom of his shirt over it. He walked over to the counter, but instead of putting it in the sink he placed the plate back in the kitchen cabinet.

Diane gave Jack a horrified look.

Chris turned around and said with a deadpan expression, "That's how we roll around here, right, Sadie?" After a few seconds, Chris looked at Diane and broke into a grin. "What? I'm just messing with you guys. I have a dishwasher and it's not Sadie!" They all laughed loudly as he took the plate out of the cabinet and set it in the kitchen sink.

"I forgot to warn you, Diane, that Chris can be a little prankster at times."

"Now you tell me. You men are all just a bunch of crazies."

"While you guys are doing your spying thing, I mean conducting your investigation, I'm going to pick up a load of gravel, so I'll have it ready to go at 6:00 a.m. on the fifth. Everyone is shutting down early for the fourth. I'm dealing with the union, and you know they're never going to work on a holiday," Chris informed them.

"That's cool. We should be back, oh, maybe by early afternoon, depending on what we find out," Jack replied.

"Sounds like a plan, my man," Chris said. "Thanks for cooking up the breakfast, Diane." Chris headed for the door. "Oh, I'd better give you my spare key. I know you'll want to lock up your stuff when you leave." He walked over to a kitchen cabinet drawer and pulled out a house key. He tossed it to Jack. "See you in a bit, master spies."

Jack gave him a salute and Diane did her princess wave as he left.

"Diane, can you find out who owns the ranch and barn in question? It might help if we know something about the owners before we just show up on their doorstep."

"Okay, give me twenty or thirty minutes. I need to hack into the Sedgwick county recorder's computer files."

"Well, you could just call and ask them, like most people." He chuckled.

"I could, but I don't want to be put on hold for twenty minutes. And don't you have something you could be doing?" she asked sarcastically.

Jack checked his emails. "Here is one from Max, Diane." He read it out loud.

Jack,

I doubt if any of this intel pertains to our investigation.

(1) Iranian sub spotted four hundred miles east, off the coast of Seattle.
(2) Pakistan puts nuclear forces on high alert after a dispute with India over water rights.

(3) Russia installs new surface-to-air missile batteries in Syria.

(4) A new Southwest terrorist cell makes contacts with Mexican drug lords.

(5) Iranian weather satellite projected to burn up in the atmosphere somewhere over North America in the next twelve hours.

If you find a connection with any of these events, call me.

Max

"I'll forward the email to you, Diane," Jack said as he thought to himself, *I'm still considering the weather satellite could be some type of EMP weapon. Even if the U.S. Space Command doesn't believe it. But what connection could Professor Kassar have with the weather satellite?*

"Diane, what did you find out about the ranch with the barn?"

"The farm was purchased in 1987 by a Roger Doerflein. He immediately built a new house on the land. He lived there until he sold it six months ago. He moved to Vegas and re-tired. Guess who brought the ranch? Are you ready?"

"Okay, who?" Jack was a little annoyed.

"Clayton Pluckbaum, the associate professor to Kassar."

"Well, the plot thickens. Damn, now I really want to see what's in that barn! Princess Warrior, you ready to go on a barn hunt?"

She grabbed her hair and pulled it into a ponytail. "Now I'm ready. Let's get that killer cow!"

* * *

9:20 a.m.

A few minutes later they drove slowly past the residence of Professor Clayton Pluckbaum.

"Doesn't look like anyone's home," Diane said.

"Time for a little visit, then." He backed up and pulled into the gravel driveway, but left the motor running. He grabbed his Glock, racked the slide, and handed it to Diane.

"Stay in the Suburban and cover me. I'm going to knock on the door just to make sure no one is home."

"Okay," she replied as she placed her trigger finger on the guard of the pistol and lowered her window. She took a deep calming breath, trying to slow her rising heart rate.

Jack hopped out and walked on a short sidewalk right up to the front door. He knocked three times, loudly. He waited a few seconds and knocked again. Still no answer. He leaned close enough to rest his ear against the door. He couldn't hear any sounds coming from inside the house.

Diane thought she saw the curtains move ever so slightly, or was it just her nerves getting the better of her?

Jack walked back to the SUV, feeling a little relieved he didn't have to explain why he and Diane were there on the associate professor's doorstep. He climbed back into the vehicle. "I think we are alone. I want to park over near the barn, as close as I can get, in case we need to make a beeline the hell out of here."

"Makes sense to me," she replied.

They pulled up to a very large barn, much older than the house on the property. Jack held his hand out. "Glock, please!"

Diane handed it to him. She reached under her seat and retrieved her pistol. She smiled. "Just in case there *is* a killer cow in there."

He returned her smile and just nodded his head.

The first obstacle they encountered was a tall, wide wooden door connected to a rail at the top. Jack slid the barn door open enough to slip in. It was dark except for thin beams of sunlight coming in from gaps in the old wood siding. There was an odd odor of old wood, dirt floor, and oil combined. In the center of the barn was a shiny metal fuel tanker trailer.

"Well, we found the right barn all right. This thing must be at least forty or fifty feet long," he said in a hushed voice.

They walked around inside the barn, looking for clues.

"Obviously, there was some kind of makeshift machine shop in here. There is a drill press, welder, and cutting torches. Looks like they moved the tanker trailers in here and cut them up for scrap. I guess you can say it pays to get rid of the evidence." Jack stepped around and over the piles of metal scraps lying on the ground.

"For the money or to get rid of the evidence?" she inquired with a lift of her brow.

"Maybe both."

"This doesn't make sense," Diane mumbled while standing at the end of the tanker. "It looks like they cut the end of the tank off. Look at these U-shaped rails. See the small rollers attached to them? And see how they're spaced evenly around the tank? You don't need any of that to haul a liquid, such as kerosene."

Jack looked over the rails, then climbed into the tank. He held his arms straight out. "Take a picture of me, Princess. This must be about eight-foot around."

She took the picture with Jack standing inside the tank, and a picture of the rails.

"Now send the pictures to Max and to Chris. I want to

know what they think."

"Roger that."

Jack hopped down from the trailer. Out of the corner of his eye, he saw the sunlight disappear and reappear on several cracks in the siding. Someone, or some*thing*, was moving toward the large sliding door.

He whispered, "We have company," and motioned to Diane to be still.

She pointed to a toolbox behind her, where she'd laid her pistol down to take the photographs. Jack quickly tucked his gun in his waistband, behind his back.

The door suddenly slid all the way open to reveal three men lined up in front of it. A motorcycle rumbled nearby, then it stopped.

"What are you doing in here, and who the hell are you?" shouted a man brandishing a gun and pointing it at Jack.

"Take it easy, my name is Jack Johnson, and this is my daughter Diane. We heard the ranch is going on the market soon and we want to put in an offer for your ranch, to raise horses. This barn would be perfect." Jack pointed to the side of the barn. "We could put six stalls over here and another six over there, right, Diane?"

By now all three men were brandishing handguns and the man asking the questions was still pointing his gun at Jack.

"I heard the woman say, 'Roger that.' That is a military phrase. You are both lying to me; you are government agents. Do you think I'm stupid? I think it's time for you to die now." He pulled back the hammer on his gun.

Jack dove on the ground, rolling over and coming up with his gun as they both exchanged gunfire. Diane launched herself forward and rolled toward the toolbox where her gun rested. The other two men were now pointing their guns in

Jack's direction. In one quick motion, she grabbed her Glock and double tapped six shots, aiming center mass at her targets. All three men fell to the ground. None of the downed men were moving.

"Jack, Jack, are you okay? Are you hit?" She could see blood dripping down the side of his face.

"I don't think so. I think I just slashed my head on some sharp-ass scrap metal here on the floor. A guy can get hurt being in here. Where's the safety manager?" Jack said, rubbing the long, but not deep, cut on his forehead.

"Let me see." She stepped over sheet metal heaped in piles on the dirt floor. "You're losing a little blood, but you still have your sense of humor." She spotted a white rag folded on a corner of a metal welders' table and applied direct pressure to his wound. "Now what do we do, Jack? Our barn hunt is now a crime scene."

He looked up at her. "The last thing we need is a bunch of cops running around here with the professor just down the road."

"I know, but we have three dead bodies here."

Jack was just getting ready to call Max when he heard a gunshot, followed by two more shots, nearby. "I think that came from the house."

By the time they made it to the barn door, they heard the roar of a motorcycle leaving the area and heading down the road in the direction of the professor's ranch. They quickly put on their bulletproof vests and drove the short distance to the house. They carried their submachine guns as they exited the SUV. The front door left standing wide open.

Jack entered first and a few seconds later he shouted to Diane, "First room clear!" She then entered the first room.

"Man down on the kitchen floor," he called as he kicked

a handgun away from the man. He continued to search the house, calling out after checking each room. Standing in the last room he called, "All clear."

He returned to the kitchen, where she was checking for vitals on the man.

"He's still alive."

Jack pulled the man over and leaned him up against the base of a kitchen cabinet. "Can you hear me?" Jack asked him.

The tall slender man with dark hair nodded his head.

"Who are you? Why were you shot?"

He answered in a very slow and weak voice, "I live here. My name is Clayton Pluckbaum."

"Why did they shoot you?" Jack repeated.

"They were afraid I'd talk. I wouldn't have."

"Why would you want to protect them now, after they shot you?"

"We are all going to die soon. It doesn't matter anymore."

"Who? How soon?" Jack demanded.

He turned his head toward Jack. There was blood running out of the corner of his mouth. He took a sharp, deep breath, then he went limp, with an empty stare.

Diane removed his dark-framed glasses and closed his eyes.

"Great," Diane said in an exasperated tone. "We now have a crime scene part two. And now one of our key persons of interest is dead."

"Don't touch anything. Call Max and tell him what took place. Tell him we do not have time to talk to the police right now. We need to get to the professor's ranch as quickly as possible. If the professor is in on it, he will be getting ready to welcome us and not in a good way," he stressed.

He searched for Clayton's cell phone and computer while

Diane placed the call to Max. After finding a cell phone and a laptop, he stashed them in the back of the Suburban. Diane was sitting in the passenger's seat with the door open, explaining what had just happened to Max.

"We are off to see the professor next. Can you send us some info on the old Air Force training center located near, or on, the professor's ranch? We believe it would have been built back in the 1960s."

Jack motioned he wanted to talk to Max.

"Max, Jack needs to talk to you. Here he is." She handed him the phone.

"I've got a bad feeling about the professor. If you don't hear anything from us in a couple of hours… call in the colonel and blow his ranch to hell."

"Are you sure that's what you want?" Max questioned.

"Yes, these people are not playing games. Shit is about to hit the fan."

"Are you requesting backup, Jack?"

"No, not yet. We need to go to the ranch to find some answers… then … maybe?"

"Good luck, Jack. Keep in touch," Max replied.

Jack started gathering all the ammo and placing it between the front seats. "Are you ready, Princess Warrior?"

"As ready as I'll ever be, Captain."

"If you know any good prayers, now is the time to say them." Jack pulled the Suburban out onto the country road. "I must say, it's been a pleasure working with you. And you look smashing in those shorts with the bulletproof vest."

"Well, thank you," Diane said, fluttering her eyelashes playfully at Jack. "I can say the same about you, including the shorts," she laughed. Her ringtone sounded. "Hi, Katia, there you are… Hey, I'll text you the address of a Chris Finley. We are staying with him at his place." She tried to make light conversation. "He has a big German Shepherd dog named Sadie who barks but doesn't bite. You should meet us there." She decided to tell Katia the truth to make sure she didn't home in on their GPS and follow them. She had the skills and equipment to do it. "We are on our way to the prime suspect's ranch. It's too dangerous for you to meet us there. Just stay at Chris's ranch and we can meet up later today." Katia tried to argue, but Diane cut her short. "See you soon. Bye." She texted Katia Chris's address. She also sent Chris a text.

Be on the lookout for my friend and co-worker Katia. She will be driving my white 2017 Mustang convertible.

Thanks, D

"Max just sent me a link about the old Air Force base. It was considered a top-secret installation. Built in the spring of 1959 and used to train Minuteman and later Atlas missile crews, it was an exact scale model of command control and launch control systems. Designed to withstand a direct nuclear blast."

"Well, hell, no wonder the professor wasn't concerned about being kidnapped. He probably has the safest home in Kansas."

"True that, Jack. Do you think he has anything to do with the weather satellite?"

"All we know is he has been conducting experiments since his retirement from the university. The one question I have is, who was he doing the experiments for… himself, or maybe some terrorist group? And why did his associate have to die to shut him up? What's the big secret?"

CHAPTER 15

July 3 at 9:50 a.m.

ROLLING DOWN THE country road, Jack noticed the Suburban was leaving a dust trail behind them. He slowed down, trying to avoid detection. Both Jack and Diane's cell phones sounded at the same time.

"It's a text from Homeland Security."

"Read it to me, Princess."

Urgent Warning: It has been disclosed the Iranian weather satellite has a nuclear-powered engine on board. A slight risk that the engine could pose a threat if it survives re-entry. Iran has given permission to shoot down the satellite if possible. Stand by for time and probable impact location. Use standard nuclear accident protocol if you are near the impact vicinity.

"What do you make of that, Jack?"

"Kind of gives my theory of the satellite containing an EMP bomb some credence."

"What about shooting it down? Why, if indeed it is a weapon? That doesn't make any sense, does it?"

"Not unless they're using our missile launch as an excuse to counterattack."

"I wouldn't shoot it down. There is a good chance it will burn up on re-entry, anyway. It could be a diversion. What if a nuke goes off in Moscow and in China just as we fire missiles at a weather satellite? All hell would break loose, right?"

"I'll call Max and give him your scenario. You, Princess, have a devious mind." He placed his index finger to his temple.

"It's just my nature," she admitted.

Jack called Max and told him about Diane's concern.

Max answered immediately. "Jack, we will shoot it down. We have notified all the countries involved of your concerns. The Air Force is happy to have an opportunity to test a new anti-satellite weapon system. I couldn't change their minds if their lives depended on it."

"Well, let's hope they're right," Jack huffed and hung up. "Sounds like we need to just focus on the professor. I don't think anyone is worried about the satellite except us." Jack gripped the steering wheel with tight fists. He had a gut feeling the satellite was going to play a big part in this mission.

"I agree, they have much more intel than we have."

"This has to be the professor's place."

They slowly drove past the entrance.

"Look, it has two lanes, and the asphalt is very old. I believe that small building was a guard shack back in the day. And it's got a fence running parallel to the road."

Jack elected not to use the main entrance. He realized he had lost the element of surprise and the professor was probably expecting them. The last thing he wanted was to drive right into an ambush. After driving about a half mile, he noticed that the fence stopped shortly before a bridge spanning a small stream.

He slowed down. "I think we can cut over here and circle back toward the professor's ranch. What do you think?" He stopped, then backed up to the end of the fence line.

"I think we'll be okay if we can squeeze between the creek and the end of the fence. Get too close to the creek and we'll get stuck for sure! And if it rains while we're out in those fields, we will be walking," she answered cautiously.

"Check the weather radar and see if there are any thunderstorms in our area."

She reviewed the weather radar on her laptop. "I don't see anything in the fifty-mile range. The forecast is a sixty percent chance of scattered thunderstorms today. The high is expected to be around eighty-nine degrees. Winds calm, ten to fifteen miles per hour. This weather update brought to you by the Princess Warrior Spy Weather Network," she replied with a grin on her face.

"You know, Diane, if we ever make it out of here alive, I can totally see you working for the Weather Channel."

She laughed. "I can see you working as a pitchman on an infomercial selling arthritic cream."

Jack gave her a wounded look. "Oh, now that's a low blow!"

"Well, it's maybe a little too late. If we fail, there might not be a Weather Channel–or any television, for that matter."

"I guess this is it, now or never. Hold on... this is going to be a bumpy ride." He eased the Suburban down into the shady ditch, barely missing a large oak tree. He stayed off the creek's edge where there was a sharp four-foot drop. The muddy creek bank had hundreds of footprints left by cattle. No doubt a favorite watering hole for the locals.

The SUV started swaying back and forth and all their gear in the back rattled and moved about.

Diane banged her head on the window. "Ouch!" She rubbed the spot.

"I told you to hold on," Jack quipped back at her.

The bottom of the Suburban dragged on some small trees as they made it uphill to a clearing.

"Hey, bumpy head, can you look at the satellite pictures and see where we are?"

"Sure, that's a great idea, just give me a minute… Here is the creek, so we must be here." She pointed to their location on the laptop. "I can see the two-lane entrance that goes back from the road. It's about a half mile, maybe. That looks like a parking lot there. I don't see any entrance going to an underground bunker."

Jack steered around a stump in the pasture. "I'm thinking he built the house on top of the entrance. That's what I would have done. It's hard to tell elevations from these photos, but I think this is a manmade hill or mound. Must be about a hundred meters from the house and seventy-five meters to those old missile silos. If we can drive over there, we'll have some cover and a good observation point."

"Indeed, Captain Jack."

The open pasture was very bumpy, but drivable. Patches of tall grass and weeds scattered among large and small rocks. The SUV was leaving an intermittent trail of bent and broken weeds. The dirt and vegetation seemed to cry as wheels rolled over it, making for a noisy ride.

"You know, Jack, when I'm in my office using metadata, I know certain factors. What I *don't* know, I can prove with data whether or not I'm on the right track. If not, then I change the factors until I get it right."

"The difference between your job and a field agent's is that what the field agent doesn't know he won't know until he or she finishes the case by winning or dying in the process."

"Well, I've never in my life been interested in losing at anything. We'll figure it out, then we'll kick their asses and go home."

Jack laughed. "The nut doesn't fall far from the tree, does it? You sound just like your dad, except with a little less profanity. I like your style, Princess, always keeping it positive.

"I think this is the hill we saw in the satellite photo." Jack maneuvered the Suburban parallel to the hill, driving alongside and stopping slightly toward the top.

"Jack, I'm sure of it."

"Let's get out and see where we are."

Diane quickly picked up her sunglasses and submachine gun, flipping the safety off. Slowly she slid out of her leather seat. Jack located his Nikon binoculars in the storage compartment between the front seats.

Up the hill the two went, crouching low to the ground, nearly crawling their way up to the top. The first thing Jack saw was an eight-foot-tall chain-link fence running along three sides of the property. The only opening in the fence was in the front of the residence, all the way to the road.

"How are we going to maneuver around the fence?"

"I think it's time to use my drone. It can bop right over the fence and take a closer look at what's happening. If they notice it, they will know we're here. But at least we have some distance between us."

CHAPTER 16

July 3 at 10:05 a.m.

DIANE LAY DOWN in the knee-high grass, looking through the binoculars while Jack retrieved his drone from the Suburban. She slowly scanned around the house and outbuildings. She saw no movement of any kind. "Looks clear to me."

"Great. Now, we only have about ten minutes of flight time before the batteries die on us. I have my drone's HD camera in sync with my laptop, so we can record the video feed."

"Did you figure that out all by yourself?" she asked, mocking his computer smarts.

"Sometimes you can be a smart-ass, Princess. I guess that's why we get along so well."

"Roger that, Captain Jack."

They both made faces at each other.

"Cross your fingers and toes, 'cause here goes nothing." He reached over and checked the connections on the drone's camera, then picked up the handheld controller.

"Jack, your phone is ringing." Before Jack could retrieve his cell phone from the Suburban, Diane's cell phone rang. "It's Max, Jack."

"Put him on speakerphone."

"Hello, Max, I have you on speakerphone."

"Max," Jack acknowledged.

"Good news… About an hour and twenty minutes ago an embedded radiation sensor in a manhole cover detected

126

radiation from a box truck that was one mile from the White House. FBI and two of our teams followed and blocked the street, just six blocks from the White House. An incident occurred, with both suspects shot. One died instantly. The other died on the way to the hospital."

Max went on with his report. "Before the suspect died, he was interrogated by one of our agents. The agent asked if he was Blackbird. He nodded his head, and then took his last breath. The FBI disarmed a ten-kiloton nuclear bomb inside the rented box truck. From the president on down, we are receiving tremendous praise for our teams, which includes you two. There is a complete news blackout on this event until we have completed our investigation. The CIA has determined the terrorists are in fact paid mercenaries. Your new orders are to wrap up your investigation on the professor and report back to Washington in the next couple of days," Max concluded.

"Max, you're kidding, right? We had four people killed just a couple of miles from us. I still don't know what the hell is going on here and you want us to pull the plug? What the hell, Max!" Jack scoffed.

"Jack, I have my orders too. A team of FBI investigators and a crime scene clean-up team are on the way to that location. Just wrap it up and I'll see you soon."

Jack frowned, but replied, "Copy that."

"What's going on, Jack?"

He hesitated. "I think the FBI is taking over the case from us. But we still have today to check out the professor. I'm not writing off our investigation just yet. My guess is the feds have somehow connected the professor to the nuke in Washington."

He started flying his drone toward the outbuilding near

the back of the two-story cement-block home, hovering only four feet off the ground, trying not to be detected.

Diane was looking at Jack's laptop screen. "What is that?"

Jack steered the drone over a flat metal cover.

"Looks like an escape hatch for the missile crews, in case of a fire."

"Can we get inside using the escape hatch?"

"No, it can only be opened from the inside. These missile sites were built to take a direct nuclear blast. Only one way in, and that is through a ten-ton steel door that he built the residence around. I don't see us getting inside unless invited."

"What about air shafts? They must have air to breathe."

"Air shafts are scattered about the premises. None large enough for a human to fit into, Princess."

Jack directed the flight of the drone over the outbuilding closest to the residence. "This was probably a maintenance building. See the two pickup trucks through the window? Oh, that's not good. The white one has an NSV Russian heavy machine gun mounted over the cab."

"Proof positive our professor is, in fact, a terrorist."

CHAPTER 17

July 3 at 10:22 a.m.

"TIME TO LOOK over the missile silos before the drone's battery dies."

Diane looked at her watch. "Eight minutes, better hurry."

He made for a straight course to the silos. The first one looked old and undisturbed.

He maneuvered the drone over the top of the other one. "This one looks different, you can tell the round door or hatch was bolted shut at one time." He moved the drone inches away from the door. "Look, Diane, you see the threads of the holes, no rust, and there appear to be some recent wide tracks left in the dirt by some kind of massive equipment."

"Are you thinking what I'm thinking?" she asked.

"Yes, it all makes perfect sense now. Somewhere in Mexico they built sections of a rocket, loaded them inside a tanker trailer, and welded up the end of the tank. Then they drove it across the border into El Paso. Then they filled up the rocket section with RP-1 Kerosene and drove it to the Professor's ranch. They cut off the end of the tank and unloaded the rocket section down into the silo at night to avoid being discovered by any satellite pictures. Then they took the tanker trailer over to the barn and cut it up into pieces and hauled it away as scrap. They must have done this several times. I bet you dimes to donuts there is a record of all this scrap at the local metal recycling center."

"I believe what you're saying. I just don't see anything we can do about it except call in the military."

"I have a feeling they're gonna launch the rocket soon, Diane!"

"What the hell is that sound?" she asked.

The sound became louder and ear-piercing.

"It's some kind of sonic weapon. Quick… let's get back to the Suburban!" Jack shouted.

They staggered down the hill, dizzy and on the verge of vomiting from the intense sound. Jack accidentally dropped his laptop and his drone crashed to the ground. They got to the Suburban and both struggled to open the door. They finally managed to climb inside.

With the noise deadened by the armor-plated vehicle, the two were feeling slightly better.

"You okay, Princess? I think we just met the professor!"

"He's a pretty rude dude if you ask me." She rubbed her ears and opened and closed her mouth like a fish out of water, trying to clear her ears.

"The navy has sonic weapons like that to keep small boats away from their ships. They're nasty but not fatal."

Jack noticed something moving in the rearview mirror. "Hang on."

She heard a loud roar. Jack now saw a white pickup speeding straight toward them.

Jack started the engine, slammed the gearshift to drive, pushed the gas pedal to the floor, and the SUV lunged over the top of the hill.

Diane reached for her submachine gun.

Jack asked her to find the smoke grenades. She located one, pulled the pin, and tossed it out her window. He noticed that the truck came down the hill and stopped a quarter of a mile behind them. Someone exited the passenger side of the truck, climbed up into the truck bed, and was now starting to fire the heavy machine gun mounted on the roof of the cab.

Seconds later, the truck disappeared into the thick cloud of smoke.

"Get ready to take a shot at the gunner. We have only one chance at this."

Jack turned the wheel sharply to his right, powered back up the hill, and drove along the top. Once on the high ground, Jack steered back toward the pickup.

Diane was leaning out the window, ready to fire at the gunner. The sonic weapon was affecting their senses more with her window down and now smoke was pouring in too. Her eyes were tearing up. She was dizzy and feeling weak, like she might pass out.

Breaking through the smoke into view was the pickup truck, downhill and to her right. A terrorist wearing headgear fired the heavy machine gun wildly into the smoke.

"Target sighted!" she shouted.

He stopped the Suburban. She was looking down her gun sights at the gunner. She fired in full-auto mode, a long burst, as the gunner fell back inside the truck bed.

The driver stumbled out of the truck with an RPG-7 and quickly fired his rocket-propelled grenade.

"RPG!" she shouted as she braced for im-pact.

The rocket's aim was low, striking the hill, but it still rolled the Suburban over on its left side.

Jack kicked out the sunroof and they both crawled out. Traces of blood trickled from their ears and noses, caused by the air pressure of the explosion. She quickly found her pistol and changed the magazine on her submachine gun.

Jack sat with his back against the roof of the Suburban and

rubbed the side of his head. He was bleeding from a cut just above the left temple he received slamming into the door-frame during the rollover. "Can you see the driver?"

"No, he's still down there. There is a good chance I hit him when I took out the machine-gunner."

He grabbed his binoculars. "There it is. See the speaker mounted on top of the pole? Over near the last building closest to us, maybe two hundred meters away."

"I see it." She aimed and fired five shots. The sonic weapon went silent.

A thud and then a blinding bright flash behind them gave the sky a pinkish hue.

"Jack, what the hell was that?"

"I have no idea, Princess. We need emer-gency backup, now." He reached for his cell phone. "The damn thing's not working, try yours."

She pulled her phone out. "It's not working either. It won't power up."

Jack was trying to get to his feet, but let out a gasp and a loud moan. He dropped back to the ground. "I think I broke my left ankle. I can't put any weight on it. Check your laptop, Diane." He crawled around to the front of the Suburban, looking down on the truck. "I see no movement around the truck."

"All the laptops are dead too, Jack. I'm not sure if the pickup is still running."

"I think we have been hit with some type of EMP device. Looks like we are stranded. The good news is they can only kill us once." Jack chuckled under his breath.

She rolled her eyes at him. "Oh, that's reassuring. Nothing better than dying with your humor intact," she said sarcastically. "What the hell are we going to do? We can't stay here. He could have a small army in the underground bunker."

Jack didn't answer. He was watching the missile silo door slowly open and slowly close. "He is doing his final countdown checklist before launching. How fast can you run five miles, Diane?"

"Maybe thirty-five minutes."

"I need you to run to Chris's ranch, and pray that he has returned home and the EMP pulse didn't go that far. Get him to drive his dump truck here. The one loaded with stone. It's our only chance. And call your dad, we need him here. Got it?"

"I'll just take my pistol with me."

"Remember what Chris said about the water tower. His ranch is a mile before it. After you get past the silos, use the water tower as a landmark, run in a straight line toward the water tower. Run wide of the fence all the way around. I'll cover you."

Now in tears, she responded, "Don't worry, I'll be back!"

She ran down the other side of the hill, away from the truck as fast as she could on the hilly terrain.

Jack watched her until she dropped out of sight. He crawled back through the sunroof opening and found the first aid box. Inside the box was a handful of auto-injectors of ten milligrams of morphine. Jack removed the red cap from one and pressed the auto-injector of mor-phine into his hip. He relaxed and five minutes later he sighed as the pain slowly started to subside.

CHAPTER 18

10:37 a.m.

SHE TOLD HERSELF to settle down and concentrate on the rough terrain in front of her.

Stepping on a rock, falling, getting hurt can cost Jack his life. He's depending on me.

She glanced back as she passed by the remaining length of the chain-link fence behind the professor's property. She tried to control her breathing and pace herself. She began thinking random thoughts.

Just a few weeks ago, I was safe and sound in my air-conditioned office, struggling to choose which flavor of espresso I'd have that day.

Why did Jack want me to move in a straight line cross country when I could cross over to the dirt road and maybe flag a motorist down?

What if I call my father and he and his Special Response Team arrive and get blown away? How will I live with myself?

I can't win. Still, there is a good chance we could all die anyway.

Thinking she was moving parallel to the road they'd driven on their arrival, she searched the skyline. One small object stood out in the landscape.

Maybe the water tower? Or maybe a big barn or a grain silo. I can't be sure. God, what do I do?

She heard an engine and figured she was near the road. The sound was gradually getting louder. She was looking to her left along the tree line, thinking the road must be on the opposite side. She looked for signs of a vehicle traveling between the trees. Nothing was visible, but the sound was getting closer. She turned around to gauge how far she had run.

Fear overcame her. She spotted a motorcycle moving straight toward her and realized the possibility that it was the same motorcycle she heard leaving after the murder of the associate professor. She guessed it was a hundred yards behind her and closing. The tree line was on her left, about two hundred yards away.

She knew she couldn't elude the motorcycle. There was no cover and nowhere to hide. The driver began firing. She realized he was too far away to be accurate. Holding his pistol in his right hand and steering with his left, he was now at fifty yards. She counted the shots as the bullets kicked up the dust around her while she ran in a zigzag pattern.

She reached into the front of her waistband and pulled out her pistol. He was now sixty feet away and stopped to get a better aim at her. She heard the motorcycle stop. Bullets whizzed by her, missing by inches–until she felt a fierce sting on her back. She was hit, and the force knocked her on the ground face-first. She rolled, stopping when she saw him between her feet at the end of her gun sights.

She double tapped four rapid shots. He went down with the motorcycle on top of his right leg. She charged at him in a low crouched position, firing three more shots. Now kneeling over him, she checked for a pulse.

He opened his eyes as he turned his head to her. "I'll kill you... you—" he groaned and rolled off his hand that was still gripping his pistol.

She pumped two more bullets in his chest. "Not now! See... it's not nice to pick on girls."

She searched for his cell phone; no such luck. She leaned the motorcycle upright to examine its condition. The front tire was flat and there were two holes in the gas tank. She laid the bike down. She unfastened her bulletproof vest, reached around with her hand, felt her back for a wound, then looked at her hand. Good; no sign of blood.

Well, I'll be damned; the damn thing works.

She fastened her vest back together and ran for the tree line. Once inside the woods, she struggled to run in a true direction, zigzagging around the thick cottonwood, elm, and oak trees. Tree branches scratched her arms, legs, and face. She tripped on several occasions over tree roots and underbrush. The trees all began to look the same, so she was not confident about her sense of direction.

Still no road, but she knew there was a road somewhere. There had to be. Fear was overtaking her. She was desperate to discover a way out of the forest. She had run for seven and a half minutes.

She knew she could have traveled at least a mile if she ran in a straight line, even in these woods.

She saw a narrow clearing up ahead. Her spirit soared with anticipation. She sprinted up a small slope. On the other side was a narrow stream encrusted with mud, leaves, twigs, small pebbles, and a trickle of water flowing toward the direction she was convinced was the professor's ranch. Feeling confident the road was near, she charged on.

Two hundred yards later she saw another clearing. This time she could see the dirt road.

There it is!

She struggled through the remaining trees. She listened to a vehicle speeding down the road. She ducked behind a large oak tree near the road to peek at the vehicle. A large flatbed truck zoomed past with eight to ten armed men riding on the back, speeding toward the professor's ranch.

Now scared for Jack, tears filled her eyes. With the truck gone from sight, she ran for help. She was feeling the heat of the sun, and perspiration poured out of her body, stinging the scratches on her face and arms. She questioned if she would have the strength to run all the way to the Finley ranch.

Please, God, send somebody down this damn road.

A few minutes later an older silver Chevy Equinox came rolling down the road.

I'm not allowing this one to get past me.

She set herself in the center of the road, swinging her arms above her head, yelling, "Stop!"

An attractive driver in her thirties rolled to a stop. She lowered her window an inch to listen to what Diane was saying.

Diane was trying to get herself under control as she moved in front of the vehicle and shouted, "Help, I'm a federal agent! I need your help, now. This is a national emergency."

The lady didn't move. She glared back at her.

Not the reaction Diane demanded. She pulled her pistol and pointed it at the lady. "Get out of the vehicle!"

The lady still did not budge, though she shouted back, "What do you want?"

Diane asked, "Do you know the way to the Finley ranch?"

The lady lowered her window some more. "Yes, but what does that have to do with a national emergency?"

"Unlock the doors, put the car in park, and put your hands behind your head."

The lady pleaded, "Please, don't hurt me. I'm a single mother."

"If you don't help me, you and everyone you know will die. Please, I'm not going to hurt you." Diane didn't want to frighten the woman, but if leaving her by the roadside got the job done, then that was what needed to happen.

The lady placed her vehicle in park, unlocked the doors, and put her hands behind her head.

Diane walked around and opened the passenger door to slide in. "What's your name?"

"Cindy D'Adamo," she answered in a trembling voice.

"Well, Cindy, do you have your cell phone with you?"

"No, I left it at home. I'm on my way to pick up my daughter."

"Okay, you can put your hands down. I need you to take me to the Finley ranch as fast as you can. Then go pick up your daughter and get as far away from Wichita as you can, as soon as possible. If Wichita is still here tomorrow, then you can come home. Seconds count… Move it or let me drive!"

Cindy slammed her gearshift in drive and made a quick U-turn to head back to Chris Finley's ranch.

"Faster, faster!" Diane shouted at her.

"Is this some kind of terrorist threat?" Cindy asked.

"I can't say anything except get your daughter and get at least three or four hundred miles away from here. Can you go any faster?"

"I'm doing eighty miles an hour. You want to get there alive, don't you?" she snapped.

"How soon till we're there?"

"One to two minutes."

"Okay, when we get within a quarter mile of the ranch, turn on your car's emergency flashers, honk your horn three short times, followed by three longer times, and continue repeating this. When we get there, pull into his driveway and drive me all the way to his front door. Got it?"

Cindy nodded her head.

Diane took a deep breath and tried to calm herself and Cindy down. "How do you know the Finleys?"

"My Jenny is good friends with their daughter, Julie. I know Chris, and he is no terrorist. He is a war hero!"

"I know, Cindy. Chris is a great friend of my partner, Jack. They served in the Middle East together. Jack and I need his help."

Cindy turned on her flashers and honked the horn as directed.

"If we live through this, I will come back and take you and your daughter out to dinner. Say a prayer for us, and thank you for helping me."

Cindy drove Diane right to the front door.

"Get away, as far as you can," Diane repeated herself and slid out of her seat, slamming the door behind her.

"What the hell is going on? Where's Jack?" Chris demanded.

Sadie was barking, adding to the commotion.

Cindy turned her vehicle around on Chris's lawn and left a trail of dust as she sped away for her daughter.

"Got any guns, Chris?" Diane demanded in a harsh voice as she walked through his kitchen.

"I have a couple AR-15s," he responded with a look of confusion.

"Perfect. Get them and all your ammo and meet me at your dump truck. Oh, I snatched your cell off the kitchen table." Diane walked out the front door on her way to the dump truck, a short distance away. She used Chris's phone to call her father.

"Colonel Glass, how can I help you?"

"Dad, we need you down here ASAP. We are at the old closed Air Force missile training center outside Wichita. Call Max and he can answer your questions. I have to go. I love you."

She climbed into the dump truck's passenger seat.

Chris ran to the dump truck and tossed his rifles on the seat. He handed Diane six magazines and a full case of cartridges. Chris hopped in the driver's seat and started the truck. "Okay, Diane–now, what the hell is going on?"

CHAPTER 19

10:42 a.m.

JACK WAS IN the prone position, looking through his binoculars. He watched a man walk out of the residence, climb on a motorcycle, and speed away on the only road in or out of the old compound.

He could see movement in the upstairs and downstairs windows of the professor's house.

There must be at least six to eight people occupying the house. Who knows how many in the old control room and underground bunkers?

He spotted the motorcycle again, driving on the outside of the fence in the open ground.

Damn, he must be going after Diane.

He quickly realized he was out of range and couldn't make the shot.

I wouldn't bet against Diane. He knew with a broken ankle he could only wait for Diane to bring help. If something happened to her, most likely he would die here on this lonely hill. It was only a matter of time before they came searching for their two men in the truck and found him too.

He thought he heard gunshots off in the distance. He said a little prayer for Diane and for himself.

I've been in tough situations before, and this one is no exception. Somehow, I always survive.

Minutes seemed like hours. The sun was beating down,

making things unbearably hot. He crawled over to find some partial shade from the sun by sitting under the front tire. Minutes later he saw a flatbed truck with armed men riding on the back. They jumped off the sides of the truck as it rolled to a stop in front of the ranch house. The driver got out and shouted orders. The men scurried around and set up in positions around the ranch house.

Why aren't they coming for me? They're either waiting to be attacked or just protecting the perimeter and planning on launching the rocket. What I wouldn't give for a working cell phone. It's been too long. If Diane didn't make it, can I shoot down a rocket with an M60 machine gun?

CHAPTER 20

11:16 a.m.

DIANE WATCHED A bead of sweat drip off Chris's chin. "Okay Chris, drive on past the entrance of the professor's ranch."

"You need to tell me when to turn and give me some warning. This truck's going sixty miles per hour. I can't stop on a dime, not hauling twenty-four tons of stone."

"When you see a small bridge, you need to turn left just before the bridge. You might have to break through the fence, give yourself more room to turn. Jack almost put us in the creek."

Diane was busy loading ammo into the magazines as she spoke.

"Okay, so why exactly do we need my new dump truck? What's the plan?" Chris demanded.

She could see the adrenalin working on Chris as his eyes darted back and forth to her and then back to the road. His hands tightly gripped the steering wheel.

"Well, to tell you the truth, I don't know. Jack said to find you and bring you and the dump truck back. I'm sure he has a well-thought-out plan of attack. We didn't have time to sit around discussing it. He thinks he broke his ankle. We were waiting for another attack. Jack said, and I quote, 'I have an idea, it's a long shot, but it might just work.' And then I left to get you." She could tell he wasn't liking what he was hearing from her.

"So, you left Jack with a broken leg, surrounded by terrorists, to find me, and now we don't even know if Jack is still alive. Hell, Diane, we could be driving right into a trap!"

"I'm not going to sugarcoat this, Chris. We believe this madman professor built a huge three-stage rocket with a large nuclear warhead. If we don't stop him and this damn rocket, millions of Americans will die, including us. It's all-or-nothing. We don't have a choice. We fight or we die!" Now wearing her brave face, she wiped the sweat from her forehead and adjusted her ponytail. "We just have to do whatever it takes until my dad arrives, got it?!"

Chris clenched his jaw and glanced at her, nodding yes.

He spotted the bridge. Knowing there was a creek, and not wanting to get stuck, he stomped on the brakes and made a hard left turn into the ditch well short of the bridge. He plowed through the fence and over two small cottonwood trees.

Both of them bounced out of their seats until their seatbelts caught them.

He quickly found Jack's tracks of bent-over weeds and ruts and followed them.

Diane rolled the window down, sat on her knees, and placed her AR-15 out the window with the barrel resting on the outside mirror.

Jack heard the sound of a motor. He took the ammo belt and quickly loaded it into his M60 machine gun. He crawled beside the front tire and aimed it in the direction of the motor sound.

Diane pointed. "There! The Suburban's over there."

Chris turned straight for the overturned vehicle. "Damn, Diane, you're lucky to be alive."

"Yeah, I know."

Jack took a deep breath. As the sound got a little closer, he could see the outline of a truck, but the sun's reflection from the windshield was blinding him.

If I go down, I'm taking as many of these sons of bitches with me as I can. Just a little closer.

He trained his gun sights on the sun-reflecting windshield.

"I don't see Jack," Diane muttered. She took a deep breath.

"I see him," Chris said. "He's down on the ground by the front tire."

"Jack!" Diane hollered.

Diane?

Jack took his finger off the trigger as he recognized the dump truck, and put his head down on the ground.

God, that was close.

He pulled himself up to a sitting position with his back resting against the front bumper.

Diane jumped out of the truck before it came to a stop at the bottom of the hill. She sprinted up the hill to Jack, laid down her AR-15, and bent down to give Jack a tight hug.

"I thought you were dead, Princess. I saw a man on a motorcycle chase after you. I heard gunshots…"

"The dude on the motorcycle couldn't han-dle this Princess Warrior." She smiled and gave him another hug. She was so glad they had made it. "I saw a truckload of men heading here; I thought they were coming after you."

"I did too, at first, then they set up defensive positions around the house. They don't seem to be too concerned with us. Like they think we're too late." Jack shrugged.

"I did get through to my dad on Chris's cell and asked for back-up."

"What did Max say?"

"I tried to call Max, but the cell phone's battery died."

"So, what is our plan, bro? Why my dump truck?" Chris asked. "I don't understand."

"The Air Force built this training center the exact same way as the real missile bases, so it's built to withstand a direct hit with a nuclear bomb." Jack straightened up a bit. "Chris, have you ever seen how they capture an alligator?"

"What the hell are you talking about, bro?" Chris asked, clearly aggravated.

"Oh, I get it," Diane spoke up. "An alligator is only dangerous with its mouth open. They sneak up from behind and tape its jaws closed, because all its power is in its closing jaw."

"I want you to put your dump truck on top of the missile silo door. Your truck is the tape on this monster's mouth," Jack instructed. "If you can, back the truck up past the first set of wheels on the hatch door. If they can raise the hatch, it will catch on the wheels and drag the truck and all twenty-four tons of stone on top of the rocket. That rocket wouldn't be going anywhere. What do you think, Chris?"

"It might work, but I don't think they will just let me drive anywhere near their missile silo. What's your Plan B?

"What was that?" Chris asked in a startled tone.

"Gunshots... I think it came from the guard shack," Diane replied.

A black Suburban accelerated toward the professor's residence as a hail of machine gun fire drew a bead on it. Smoke streamed out of the radiator and engulfed the entire vehicle. Finally, the fire reached the gas tank and it exploded, flames shooting at least thirty feet into the sky.

A feeling of sadness and despair overcame the three. This was their back-up, coming to save them. They were possibly their friends, and not knowing who was in the Suburban only added to their anxiety.

Chris was now pacing back and forth behind their Suburban.

"Chris, do you carry tie-down straps and a pry bar in your truck?" Jack asked urgently.

"Most truckers carry those items, so yeah, I have them. You thinking about Plan B?"

"This Suburban has armor plating in the doors. If we can remove them and put them on your truck, your odds of surviving go up. Using the straps, we can roll the Suburban upright."

"I'm on it. Come on, Diane!"

The two of them ran down the hill to the dump truck to retrieve the straps and pry bar.

Jack watched the black smoke rise into the sky from the burning vehicle. High above he saw a silver object. It had a Y-shaped tail section. He knew the object was a new MQ-9 Reaper Air Force drone. Probably unarmed while flying over American soil. Max had to be watching.

Chris made short work tearing the tailgate off using a six-foot-long pry bar. Diane used Jack's hunting knife to cut the thick rubber molding holding the bulletproof rear window in place. They removed a large ballistic steel armor plate and rested it inside the cab of the dump truck, between the door and the driver's seat.

Diane retrieved a roll of duct tape from the Suburban and

began taping the bulletproof window on the outside of the dump truck's driver's side door window. Chris removed two more ballistic steel plates.

"Okay, Jack, what's next?" Chris asked.

Jack glanced at Diane. "Can you drive that pickup down there?"

"I can drive anything with wheels. I once drove an M1 Abrams tank around Fort Benning," she bragged.

"I think our time is running out. Chris, take my bulletproof vest. Diane, you take the sunroof and a metal plate and put it in Chris's truck. Chris, you drive down beside the pickup and give Diane cover. Tape the sunroof on the outside of the driver's side window on the pickup. Put one plate down by her feet, the other behind the seat as high as you can get it to stay.

"Shit, is that what I think it is?" Jack asked, looking at the slightly open hatch on the missile silo. "Is that white cloud liquid oxygen seeping out?"

"Yes, I think it is," Diane confirmed with a look over the hood of the Suburban.

"We gotta go, now! Chris, you drive the dump truck. Diane, you drive the pickup. You guys get me down there in the back of that truck bed and I will keep them busy so you both can drive."

"How soon before you think they intend to launch?" Chris asked with extreme agitation.

"They are bleeding off liquid oxygen from the rocket. This is the very last step. That means three minutes or less to lift-off."

Chris ran to the dump truck as fast as he could, jumped in, and drove up to where Jack was sitting. Diane helped Jack hobble into the cab of the dump truck. She handed him both submachine guns, the M60 machine gun, and the last two boxes of ammo. She grabbed the roll of duct tape and slid it over her wrist, then grabbed the sunroof. She ran down the hill holding the bulletproof sunroof as a shield in front of her.

Jack shook his head. "I'm sorry we got you into this, Chris."

"Don't say it, bro. It's life or death and I'm fighting for my wife and kid."

"Well, let's not let them down."

Chris rolled up parallel to the pickup, giving Jack cover as he hopped out of the cab on one foot.

Diane took the heavy steel plates and set one in the back of the pickup bed. "This one is yours, Jack."

He crawled on his knees into the truck bed. "Thanks, Princess." He took the plate and rolled the dead terrorist up against it.

Diane set the steel plate between her seat and the door, shielding her legs and feet and an area up to the bottom of the window, while sitting in a blood puddle from the killed driver. She laid her pistol down beside her, then pressed her head and shoulder against the sunroof, pinning it against the inside driver's side window.

Jack yelled at Chris, "We'll give you a fifteen-second head start and then pick you up!"

"Roger that." Chris stomped on the gas pe-dal.

An adrenaline high surged through Chris's veins as he tried to focus on a section of the fence. He had to take out enough of the fence so Diane could follow.

Bullets began to hit the truck, sounding like a hail storm.

CHAPTER 21

July 3 at 11:42 a.m.
Washington, D.C.

MAX UPDATED THE general. "Thank you, General Frakes. We are watching the drone's video feed as we speak. Because we have two FBI agents presumed dead and two of my other field agents missing, I am sending this video feed over to the White House Situation Room as a declared terrorist act in progress. I have Special Ops Commander Colonel Glass and two of his Special Response Teams, Silver and Blue, inbound, only minutes away."

"I located another Reaper MQ-9 drone and it's re-routed and inbound to the location; let me know if there is anything else I can help you with, Max."

"Thank you, General. I hope for a speedy resolution of this event."

"Colonel, Max here. I have a live video feed from a drone above the old Air Force training center. I wanted you to know, before I share the video feed with you, that the burning vehicle is not Diane and Jack's, but two FBI agents' I called in for back-up. There is a lot of ground activity. The whereabouts of Diane and Jack are still unknown. We are sharing this video feed with the White House. As you know, they are monitoring all communications."

"Thanks, Max, the video feed will allow us to make a threat assessment and to pinpoint a landing zone. And... I appreciate your concern for Diane."

"I'm on my way to the White House. Keep in touch! Just as you care about your men under your command, I feel the same about my investigators. We want to bring them home safely. Good luck, Colonel, and Godspeed."

CHAPTER 22

11:45 a.m.

KATIA LOOKED AT the phone's GPS.

This must be the place.

She pulled into the long empty driveway. She saw a German Shepherd sitting on the porch, watching the Mustang closely. She opened the car door and the dog lunged off the porch, running with its head and tail down.

"Sadie, hi, Sadie," she said in a high-pitched voice.

Sadie stopped within five feet of her and stared.

"Hi, pretty Sadie," she said again in the same high-pitched voice.

This time Sadie began to wag her tail.

"Where are your daddy, Diane, and Jack? Huh, Sadie?" Katia walked up to the porch and sat down.

It feels so hot, it must be a hundred degrees in the shade.

The sun was really beating down as she looked up. Not a cloud in the sky, only a little stream of black smoke rising in the distance. She saw Sadie's water bowl was almost dry. She reached over and picked up the bowl, then went to the door and knocked. No sign of anyone home. The front door was slightly ajar.

"Hello, is anybody home?"

She entered slowly, looking for the kitchen or a bathroom to fill the dog's bowl. She found the kitchen first. She thought it was kind of creepy being in a stranger's house. She filled the bowl and walked out the way she came in. Five feet from the door she stepped on something. She looked down, and under her foot was a large cartridge. Not the size you would use in a handgun, but large enough for a high-powered rifle.

She reached down to pick up the cartridge and saw three more scattered across the floor. She had an unsettled feeling in the pit of her stomach.

Someone must have been in a hell of a big hurry if they dropped ammunition while running out the door.

She was fearful for Diane. She quickly set Sadie's water bowl down on the porch. "Here, Sadie, come and get a drink."

She called Diane's cell, which went straight to voicemail. Her intuition told her Diane was in grave danger. She stepped off the porch and looked around, noting that nothing else seemed out of the ordinary. She quickly walked around to the back of the house. There were three chairs and two small tables, one with a few empty beer cans neatly stacked.

Where could they be?

She decided to call her boss, Karen Waters, just in case Diane checked in with her. Karen informed her that she hadn't talked to her since she requested some satellite pictures eighteen hours ago.

With no leads to go on, she decided to investigate the black column of smoke off in the distance.

CHAPTER 23

12:14 p.m.

MAX RUBBED HIS right temple and reached for his coffee cup, his fifth of the day. He knew this was going to be a very long one, no doubt stretching into the night. He and he alone ordered two FBI investigators for backup without knowing the risks, and that resulted in their deaths. There would be an investigation into his decision. Especially since he lost all communications with Agents Jacobs and Glass. All he had was the video feed from the MQ-9 Reaper drone flying high above the professor's ranch. Somewhere down there were Diane and Jack.

Max could see movement around the outside of the professor's residence. There appeared to be an attack on the residence. Max wished he had control of the camera which was focusing only on the residence, but that may not mean they were still alive.

He noticed a small white flash in the lower left corner of the screen, then a few seconds later the screen went black. Seconds after that, the phone rang.

"Max, General Martin here, in the Situation Room. My weapons analyst believes a shoulder-fired Stinger missile just took out our drone. Question... is Colonel Glass still inbound with two Black Hawks? I want my men out of the sky, Max! Abort the mission or ground them immediately! Do you understand? I won't lose two Special Ops teams."

"Yes, sir."

Max called Colonel Glass on his cell. "Jim, I have been ordered by the Joint Chief of Staff to abort the mission or ground the Black Hawks immediately. We believe our drone was shot down by a Stinger missile. You could be flying into an ambush. Do you copy?"

"You are breaking up, Max. Be advised we are setting down three miles northwest of the training center. We will proceed on foot from there."

CHAPTER 24

12:20 p.m.

"CAPTAIN, WE HAVE been ordered to set down as quickly and as safely as possible. The target location is believed to have obtained some Stinger missiles. Apparently, they shot down our MQ-9 drone," Colonel Glass informed the pilot.

"Roger that, Colonel. Greenbean10, this is SNAFU-9er, redirecting LZ. Stay on my six, over," said the captain.

"Copy that, SNAFU-9er," replied the pilot in Greenbean10.

The Black Hawks descended to fifty feet above the ground, three miles northwest of the professor's ranch, at an airspeed of one hundred seventy-three miles per hour.

Colonel Glass leaned his six-foot-two body in between the pilot and copilot. "Captain, can I get an open mic channel for here and Greenbean10? I want to talk to both squads at the same time if that's possible."

"Yes, sir, Colonel, just give me a second." The captain radioed Greenbean10. "Turn on your intercom and keep this channel open, the colonel wants to address both squads."

"Roger that, SNAFU-9er."

The captain took off his headset and handed it to the colonel. "All yours, sir."

The colonel placed the headset on, pressed the mic button. "Okay, men, listen up. Our mission comprises two parts. The first part is to eliminate all possible terrorist threats. Our intel is… weak to say the least. The target area was once an Air Force missile training center, back in the nineteen sixties. The Air Force underground bunker complex wasn't completely gutted when they closed the training center. There is now a ranch house built on top of where the entrance of the underground bunker is located.

"The first objective is seizing the ranch house and miscellaneous buildings. Gain entry to the bunkers and neutralize all threats. According to intel, there was the following below the ground: two classrooms, two launch control rooms, two living quarters for the missile crews, a data center, HVAC rooms, two missile silos, and interconnecting tunnels. Of course, we have no idea what they are using these rooms for or what is in them. Intel suggests as few as eight or as many as fifty persons on the premises. We believe they could be heavily armed. Intel reports suggest they shot down an Air Force MQ-9 drone with a Stinger missile.

"Therefore, our LZ now has been changed. With the threat of the Stinger missiles, we will start our advance from farther away. We cannot put our Black Hawks at risk. Once on the ground, spread out and stay three to five meters apart. Our target area is one and a half to two miles away. Our rules of engagement are to return fire and take out all threats by any means necessary.

"The second part is a search and rescue mission. Two FBI investigators are believed to be KIA." The colonel's voice cracked with emotional strain. "Two other federal agents are missing and unaccounted for. One is my daughter, Diane, twenty-eight years old, blonde, blue eyes. Her partner, Jack Jacobs, in his fifties, dark and gray hair. Possibly a third person named Chris, no other info available on him."

The soldiers were studying the colonel and hanging on

his every word.

A lieutenant spoke up. "Don't worry, Colonel. We'll find her."

All the soldiers responded with "Hooah!" and like an echo, "Hooah!" could be heard over the speaker coming from the other Black Hawk.

"Colonel, we are hovering over the LZ," the pilot announced.

"Set her down, captain," replied the colonel. "Get ready to disembark."

The colonel leaned in to the pilot. "Once we secure the training center, come in and pick up any wounded. Come in low and keep your eyes peeled. They could have defenses set up on the outer perimeter."

"Roger that, Colonel."

CHAPTER 25

JACK COULD SEE the tracer bullets converge on the dump truck. He realized why they shot down the drone. They did not want any video evidence of the rocket firing from the silo.

Diane was counting in her head, *A thousand twelve, a thousand thirteen*. "Hold on, Jack!" she yelled. She stomped on the gas pedal and began following Chris.

Jack struggled to regain his balance as Diane accelerated the old white pickup. He quickly braced himself and began firing the M60 machine gun. He was trying to slow down the rate of fire on the dump truck, and it appeared to be working. Some tracer bullets flashed past him and some hit the pickup. Jack ducked his head down as bullets landed all around him. Only the steel plate and dead terrorist in front of him stopped the bullets from ripping into him.

Diane let out a loud gasp.

Jack yelled, "Are you hit? Are you okay?"

Two bullets hit the driver's side at the same time, one in the door and one in the window. If it hadn't been for the steel armored plate and the bulletproof sunroof she pinned against the window, she knew she would have been dead. She felt and saw the impact shatter the window completely and leave a four-inch diameter fracture in the bulletproof glass sunroof.

"I'm okay. Just a jolt to my head!" she yelled over her shoulder.

Jack returned fire, spraying bullets in the direction of the terrorists' dug-in positions. He felt a sudden vibration.

"The front tire just blew. I don't know if we are going make it!" she hollered.

"All that matters is that the rocket must be stopped from launching. It doesn't matter if we die in the process, as long as the rocket dies with us."

"It matters to me, Jack! I'm not interested in dying today. You got the wrong girl!" she shouted back.

Sweat dripped off Chris's chin as he down-shifted, slowing his dump truck. It was his pride and joy. He went into debt to buy his one-hundred-seventy-five-thousand-dollar truck. He remortgaged his ranch to be able to make the purchase, which caused a huge dispute with his wife and a likely divorce. When this was all over, he was counting on restitution for his loss. He had to smile at his thoughts. *If* he was still alive after this was all over.

The smell of burning diesel fuel and oil began to fill the cab. He tried not to choke as he saw steam rolling from the radiator. Bullets riddled his livelihood, his future. Anger boiled up and consumed his soul. From a small jagged piece of the side mirror that remained, he saw the pickup truck, with Diane and Jack inside, speeding toward him. He glanced down at his temperature gauge, now pegged in the red. A strong acid smell entered the cab, and he realized his battery was shot to pieces. He slammed his fist on the steering wheel. If the engine died, he would too.

He saw the hatch door, perfectly round with two large hydraulic cylinders connected to the hinge. It was much larger than he imagined. It was between twelve and fifteen feet across.

Chris saw the hatch was still slowly opening. The only way to drive on top of it was to drive on the hinge side first.

THE BLACKBIRD THREAT

Bullets converged on the truck as Chris circled around to the hinged side of the hatch. The power steering was out, and the left front flat had him driving on the tire rim. It took all his strength to maneuver the beast. He held his breath as he turned to expose the unprotected side of the truck cab. Two bullets hit the passenger door and window, striking the radio in the dash. The windshield glass exploded inside the cab.

Chris yelled a battle cry and stomped on the gas pedal.

All the guns began to fire on the dump truck to stop him from reaching the hatch.

He didn't hear the hail of bullets hitting the truck. His world was now in slow motion as he crashed onto the hatch. The back of his head slammed near the top of the cab, nearly knocking him unconscious.

The truck came to a screeching halt with the front hanging off the opposite side of the hinge. Still dazed, he fumbled for the keys, set the emergency brake, and reached for his AR-15.

Diane shouted, "I don't see him, Jack!" She drove closer to the dump truck. "I'm afraid he will burn up in the truck."

"Looks like ten unfriendlies are less than a hundred yards away and closing," Jack warned. He fired a long burst in their direction to slow them down. The terrorists returned fire. Bullets now hit the pickup as well as the dump truck.

"You cover me, Jack. I'm going to get Chris out of that truck."

"Okay, Princess. We have maybe two minutes. Hurry!"

Again, Jack fired a long burst at the terrorists, who were now seventy-five yards away.

Diane slid over and out the passenger side door. Crouching behind the front tire, ready to run to Chris's truck, she saw Chris starting to run toward her.

Chris leaned low, took three steps, and twisted sideways, landing on his back. Blood squirted from his left thigh. He crawled on his back, pushing off with his good leg, toward the dump truck.

Diane crouched low and scurried between the two vehicles. "Take my hand."

Chris grabbed her hand, and she dragged him to the rear wheels. His back now against the tire, he moaned as he put direct pressure on his gunshot wound.

"Give me your belt," Diane ordered.

"I'm not wearing one," he replied.

She could feel his pain by looking at his contorted face. "Me neither." Concerned he might go into shock and bleed out. "I think the bullet nicked your femoral artery. I'm not sure if it hit the bone," she said, trying not to look alarmed. She quickly put her hands under her shirt, slid the bra straps off her shoulders, and pulled it down with a twist. She unhooked it, quickly folded it, placed it under his thigh, and pulled up on both sides while she tied a knot.

She looked around for something to twist for a handle of the tourniquet. She grabbed her Glock and released the magazine, then tied a knot around it. She started twisting until she saw the blood stop flowing.

"Hurry up, Diane, fifty yards!" Jack yelled.

"If we make it out of here alive, you owe me a gift card from Victoria's Secret, Chris."

"Deal," he replied. His voice was getting weak.

"Can you hold on to this?" She put his hand on the magazine.

"Yeah."

"Don't lose it, I may need it back. We've got to go. Can you stand?"

"I don't know."

"Okay, I'll drag you while you push with your good leg." She turned to yell over her shoulder, "Jack, we're going to need some cover! How many unfriendlies are left?"

"Eight!"

"Shoot better, Jack, shoot better," she countered. "You ready, Chris?"

He clenched his teeth and nodded his head.

"Okay, Jack, let them have it, we're coming over."

Jack loaded the last ammo belt for the M60.

Diane was barely off the ground as she struggled to drag the much heavier Chris over the knee-high prairie grass.

She stopped halfway to re-grip Chris's sweaty left hand. His right hand was holding on tightly to his tourniquet. Bullets hit all around them.

Jack fired the last of his ammo and the machine gun stopped. He yelled, "Out of ammo, switching to MP-7!" Jack fired two quick bursts and two terrorists went down.

Diane reached for the bumper of the pickup and pulled Chris to safety, using the pickup as cover. "You have to help me get you in the cab. I need you to stand with your back toward the seat. I'll get in first and, when I tell you, you push off with your good leg and I'll pull you in." She wrapped her arms under his and around his chest. "Ready, set, push!"

Chris gasped for air as the pain jolted his body.

"We're back, Captain Jack. Can we get the hell out of here now? Chris is bleeding pretty bad."

"My first aid kit is in the back of the Suburban. Back up the way you came so we can keep our armored side facing them," Jack ordered. He was still firing short bursts in the direction of the terrorists.

"Roger that," she replied as she slammed the gear shift

into reverse. "Lie down, Chris, and hold on. It's going to be a rough ride."

She stomped on the gas pedal and the engine roared. The pickup started to move slowly away and picked up speed even with the right tire gone and driving on the rim. She used her head and shoulder again to pin the bulletproof sunroof against the door frame. Chris flinched and moaned after each bump on the prairie landscape. She looked in the rearview mirror for the opening in the fence.

"Diane, a little more to the passenger side… That's good," Jack directed.

The bullets striking the pickup had finally stopped. Diane maneuvered the truck through the fence opening. She looked down at Chris. "Jack, Chris doesn't look very good. He has lost a lot of blood and is very pale."

"Is he cold and clammy to the touch?"

"Yes, he is, and he's kind of out of it."

"Stop the truck. Let's get him back here. He's going into shock.

She stopped the truck with the engine running. She hopped out and ran around to the back of the truck to lower the tailgate. She stepped around to Chris's side and opened the door. Reaching in, she pulled Chris upright from the blood-soaked seat. "Chris, can you hear me? I'm going to try to carry you on my back. If you can, hold on to me. This will probably hurt like hell." She turned her back to him, grabbed his arms, and leaned over with him draped across her. She moved slowly to the truck bed.

"Jack, grab his shoulders… Watch his head," Diane instructed. She leaned back and set Chris on the tailgate.

Jack checked Chris's vitals. "His pulse is weak. If he's not in shock, he is damn close. We need to elevate his legs."

She dragged the dead terrorist over and placed Chris's legs on the body's back.

"Let's get back to the Suburban. I have a first aid kit stashed in the back."

"Roger that, hold on."

She stepped around to the side, grabbed the steering wheel, and pulled herself into the cab. She slammed the door, shifted into first gear, and stomped on the gas pedal. The engine sputtered. She pumped the gas pedal to keep the engine running.

Chris blinked.

"Hey, buddy, you had me worried for a minute."

"I don't feel so good, bro," Chris muttered softly.

"You did lose a lot of blood. We're going back to the Suburban, where I have a first aid kit. You did great! You just disabled a missile silo that was designed to withstand a nuclear bomb, but not your dump truck," he said, still assessing his condition.

Diane shouted, "Hold on, Jack!" She downshifted and stepped on the gas pedal, driving up the grassy hill. The engine began to sputter. "Get your ass up this hill, you damn piece of junk... Come on, baby, come on," she coaxed the truck.

Jack reached over to grab Chris as he began to slide on the truck bed. "Hold on, buddy, almost there, just a few more seconds."

Diane parked the pickup behind the Suburban, using it as a shield. She slid out of her seat soaked in blood. She took a moment to check herself. No serious injuries.

The blood must have come from the terrorist driver and Chris.

"What's the plan, Captain?"

"Inside the Suburban is an army medic first aid kit. Can

you get it for me? Oh, and look and see if I left a jacket or windbreaker in there too."

She crawled in from the back of the Suburban. She quickly found the first aid kit, a full magazine for the submachine gun, and another full magazine for her Glock 22.

She handed Jack the first aid kit. "I didn't see any jacket."

He opened the case and took out an auto-injector of morphine. He removed the red tip and injected Chris in his left hip. After a few minutes, he could see Chris relaxing as the morphine started to take effect. He took some gauze and stuffed it into Chris's wound. He wrapped his leg several times with tape. "Hey, Diane, can you get me an ink pen or marker out of the Suburban?"

She retrieved a marker.

He wrote *MS10MG* and the time on Chris's forehead. Jack noticed she had a puzzled look on her face. "Morphine Sulfate… he can't have another dose for three hours." Jack looked at her. "When you lose that much blood, your core temperature drops. It's a hundred degrees out here and he feels cold to me. Help me take the shirt off the dead guy."

"Okay, you hold Chris's legs up and I'll swipe this guy's shirt."

Jack moaned as he hit his ankle against the wheel well inside the truck bed.

She unbuttoned the long dark gray shirt. "What do they call this type of shirt, with a long tail down past the knees?"

"It's called a *kurta.* I'm hoping we can fold it in half and double the thickness."

For the first` time Diane saw firsthand what kind of damage a bullet did to the human body. She saw the three small entrance and large exit wounds she caused. Those were her fatal shots that killed the terrorist.

She finally pulled the *kurta* over his head and off his body. Wiping the blood off her hands on the *kurta*, she folded it in half and laid it on top of Chris's chest.

"We have to get him to a hospital. I think he's in shock. He may only have an hour to live. Diane, can you locate my binoculars? I think I might have left them on the ground in front of the Suburban."

"Here they are." She retrieved the binoculars and gave them to Jack.

He hopped on his good leg to the front of the truck bed and climbed on top of the cab to get a better view.

"Any sign of the colonel?"

"They know he's coming, because they are massing on the other side of the ranch. They're coming out of the escape hatches like ants. Must be fifty or sixty of them."

"Damn, Dad's walking into a trap. We have to warn him!"

"They train for ambushes all the time. Your dad commands the best-trained soldiers in the world. Never bet against a Special Ops team, Diane."

CHAPTER 26

KATIA STRUGGLED TO see the distant pillar of smoke behind a row of trees lining the country road. She left a cloud of dust behind her, driving with the pillar of smoke on her left until she found its source. She had a sick feeling something terrible was happening. She reached in the storage compartment between the front seats for Diane's pistol and placed it beside her. Coming up on a stop sign, she turned on her emergency lights and ran the stop sign. Seconds later she heard a siren. A sheriff's car appeared in her rearview mirror and closed fast. She slowed down and pulled over to the side of the road. The sheriff's car was inches away from her back bumper as it pulled in behind her.

A tall slender sheriff's deputy got out, walked up, and put both hands on the driver's side door. "Do you know why I pulled you over, ma'am?"

Katia took her hands off the steering wheel to pull her government ID card out of her purse.

The deputy saw Diane's pistol and pulled his gun. "Freeze! Do you have a carry permit for that gun?"

"No, the gun is my coworker's, and this is also her car. She is overdue and I'm looking for her. We work for the NSA, doing a joint operation with Homeland Security." She handed him her ID card. "She is investigating a retired professor as a person of interest. He has a ranch close by. Do you know of such a person?"

He studied her ID card.

"Look, this is a possible national emergency, either you help me or get the hell out of my way!" she shouted.

He handed her back the ID. "Follow me, Katia."

The deputy returned to his squad car, turned on his lights and siren, and started to go around Diane's car.

Katia whipped the steering wheel sharply and came up beside the deputy's car. "No siren and lights. We must not give them any advance notice that we are coming, and stay off the radio, as well," she said forcefully.

The deputy turned off his lights and siren.

She let him lead the way. She backed off driving too close behind him as clouds of dust rolled into the convertible, choking her.

Minutes later she could see the waning pillar of smoke as they closed in on its location. A thin layer of dust clung to her sweaty skin. Her stomach was in knots with worry for Diane and now, for the first time, herself.

The deputy's car slowed to a stop. In front of the squad car was a homemade sign that stated, 'road closed.' It hung on two sawhorses, with landscaping timbers leaning against each set. He got out of the car and surveyed the area. There was no reason for the road to be closed. He glared back at Katia, his expression seeming to say, *What the hell is really going on?*

He slid the sawhorses over enough to drive around them.

Fifty yards farther down the road, the deputy signaled a left turn into a two-lane road. She followed him so closely that, as she turned, she almost touched his rear bumper. Seconds later a young man darted in front of the deputy's car, waving for him to stop.

The deputy stopped and immediately got out of the squad car to talk to the young man.

Katia, unsure what was happening, reached over and picked up Diane's pistol. She struggled to rack the slide, cocking the gun.

The young man told the deputy, "My uncle's car caught fire. It might explode. It is not safe to be here. You shouldn't go any farther. Maybe you could go for help?"

"Hold on, son, I'll dispatch the fire department." The deputy walked back to his car, then suddenly turned to the young man. "Is that gunfire I hear?" The deputy instinctively placed his hand on top of his holstered sidearm.

"My four cousins are rabbit hunting."

"They must be lousy shots, or you have a lot of rabbits." The deputy looked concerned and a bit wary.

He kept his eye on the young man as he walked back to the squad car. He opened the car door, reached in, and grabbed the mic on the police radio. He pressed the button on his handset. "This is Deputy Ron Iverson. I'm requesting a fire truck to be dispatched for a vehicle fire out here at—" He felt a searing pain in his left shoulder blade as a knife entered all the way down near his left lung and twisted free.

Katia fired five rounds at the young man holding the hunting knife. He fell back against the deputy's open door, sliding down to the ground in a sitting position with his mouth open.

She flung her door open and ran to the deputy. He was coughing up blood and having a difficult time breathing. Blood was seeping from his back wound.

"We must get out of here before the others come for us," she said. She helped the deputy off the car door that he'd grabbed to stay upright. They walked hunched over as he struggled for air on the way back to Diane's Mustang. He stumbled into the backseat and lay on his side.

She jumped into her seat and saw five men running toward her, carrying assault weapons. As she shifted the car into reverse, she looked in the rearview mirror to see a semi truck, pulling a long flatbed trailer, carrying a large object covered with tarps. It was turning in behind her and blocking her escape route.

Now desperate to escape the gunfire, she drove around the deputy's car and made a right-hand turn into an open field. Bullets zinged through the air before some found their mark. She told the deputy to hold on.

She leaned low over the steering wheel, until she could barely see the field with her left eye, and floored the gas pedal. The engine roared. Her knees bounced off the bottom of the steering wheel, and driving over the bumps and rocks sent her out of her seat. She saw one bullet rip through the passenger seat and into the dashboard. She kept her head down and peeked between the bucket seats to check on the deputy.

"Hey, Jack, that's Katia! That's my car!" Diane jumped up and down, waving her hands at her friend.

"She can't see you. Flash the lights and honk the horn."

Katia heard the sound of a horn honking, but all she saw was an eight-foot-tall chain-link fence coming at her, fast. She turned left wildly, away from the fence, almost rolling the car over. She glanced back between the seats to make sure the deputy wasn't ejected. He was still coughing up blood.

He's going to die right here in the car.

She stopped hearing gunshots coming in her direction. She peeked over the dash and saw Chris's dump truck and an opening in the fence. Even without knowing where the opening in the fence led, she dashed through it. Better there than sitting out in the open on this side of the fence.

Once on the other side, she could see where the honking sounds were coming from. She drove toward the honking through deep prairie grass and weeds. She was hoping it was Diane and Jack and not more of the gun-wielding assailants. At least they weren't shooting at her.

She increased her speed, knowing the deputy was in serious condition. Finally, she saw Diane jumping up and down, waving. Elated to find Diane alive and well, tears of joy trickled down her cheeks. She flashed her headlights back.

"Things are looking up, Jack." Diane beamed. She jumped down from the top of the pickup truck just as Katia powered up the hill and slammed on the brakes, parking beside the Suburban.

"He needs help, Diane." She pointed to the backseat "This is Deputy Iverson. He was giving me an escort to the ranch when we stopped at the guard station. The deputy was attempting to use his radio when a young man came up and stabbed him in the back. I shot the man before he could stab him a second time. He's coughing up blood and having a hard time breathing." Katia was fighting back panic.

"Are you alright?" Diane asked anxiously, looking over at her friend.

"Yeah, but I shot him..." Katia's voice quavered. "I shot the guy who knifed the deputy." Tears sprang into her eyes. "I killed him."

Diane held her friend as she watched Jack hobble over to check the deputy's injury.

"Quick, Diane, get me some tubing off the pickup truck engine... Try the tube from the windshield washer fluid tank. And some duct tape," Jack barked.

Diane gave Katia a quick squeeze. "Help me, okay? In the pickup cab is a roll of duct tape. Can you get that for me?"

Jack whipped out his pocket knife and started to cut the deputy's shirt off him.

Katia found the duct tape. She gasped at all the bullet holes in the vehicle and wondered how anyone could survive this.

"Got it, Jack." Diane handed him the tubing.

He took a morphine auto-injector and gave the deputy an injection. "Good news is this will help with the pain. The bad news is we don't have time for it to take effect." He took an alcohol wipe from a sealed packet and wiped the tubing several times. By now the deputy was wheezing and turning blue.

"Deputy, this is going to hurt like a son of a bitch, but only for a few seconds," Jack warned. "Okay, ladies, I need you to hold him still."

Diane looked at Jack. "Are you up to this, Jack?"

"He is going to die if I don't do something!"

Katia and Diane both grabbed ahold of the deputy on opposite sides.

Jack looked the deputy in the eye. "Okay, I need you to take in a deep breath, if you can, and hold it."

The deputy nodded his head and tried to do as instructed.

Jack started pushing the tubing inside the knife wound. He listened to the tubing, holding it against his ear. When he heard a gurgling sound, he put the tubing in his mouth and sucked. Blood filled his mouth. He spat out the blood. Blood started to flow out of the tubing.

When he saw the blood flow slow down, he quickly kinked the end of the tubing. "Okay, you can breathe now, Deputy."

The deputy coughed and took a deep breath of air. His color quickly started to return to normal.

Jack left the tube inserted in the wound and used the duct tape to cover it and hold the tube in place. He wrote *MS10MG* and the time on the deputy's forearm.

With the morphine kicking in and the blood out from around his lungs, the deputy was breathing much easier.

Diane looked at Jack with admiration. "That was slick. Where did you learn how to do that?"

"Well, where I learned is still classified. Let's just say I stayed at the Holiday Inn Express."

They laughed with pent-up adrenaline.

CHAPTER 27

"KATIA, I NEED your cell phone to call Max. We think the professor set off a small EMP device. None of our cells and laptops work."

"That explains why, when I called you, it went straight to voicemail. I knew something bad was happening!"

"Max, it's Diane… I'm okay. We're sure Jack has a broken ankle. We also have a deputy with a stab wound in the back, and Jack's friend with a terrible gunshot wound in the leg. All stable for now, but we could sure use a medevac. Is there a Black Hawk from the SRTs available?"

"The Black Hawks have been grounded a few miles away until the SRTs neutralize all unfriendly ground forces. We estimate another ten minutes before the birds can fly. Can you give us your location?"

Diane began searching inside the Suburban. "We will signal the Black Hawks with a green smoke grenade when we see them airborne. We are on the other side of the ranch, up on a hill a couple hundred meters from the perimeter security fence. The deputy and Chris are in bad shape. Please hurry!" she pleaded.

"I'll forward your intel, Diane. Hang in there. Call me back when you're in the air," Max replied.

"Roger that, sir," she replied and ended the call. "Katia, do you have any bottled water in the car?"

"No, but I do have a bottle of root beer."

"Great, see if Chris can drink some. He's lost a lot of

blood."

"Max said help will be here in ten to fifteen minutes, God willing. Did you bring a jacket or a blanket with you? Chris's core temperature is dropping."

"I'll get my suitcase." Katia ran for the trunk of the Mustang.

"Hey, Diane, come and look at this," Jack called while sitting on the hood of the pickup truck and looking through his binoculars at the colonel's SRTs.

She sat next to him on the hood. He handed her the binoculars for a look. She watched as her dad's Special Ops teams pushed the terrorists back to the first outbuilding.

"Way to go, Dad." She beamed. She looked at the silo and then back to the ranch house. "Whiskey Tango Foxtrot, you've got to be kidding," she mumbled. She handed Jack the binoculars and pointed at an object moving away from the large truck and trailer Katia told them about.

Jack took the glasses and zeroed in on where Diane was pointing. "It's heading for the silo. That is the largest bulldozer I have ever seen." Metal studs protruded around its very large steel wheels, and a huge metal blade stuck out in front. It was huge and mean-looking. Jack stared intently at Diane. "We have to kill this monster. Your dad can't get to it before it reaches the silo."

Diane tossed the green smoke grenade to Katia. "Set it off when you see a helicopter. Jack and I have some unfinished business to take care of." Diane grabbed her gun off the seat of the Mustang. She checked and made sure the magazine had some ammo remaining and handed it to Katia. "Shoot anyone not wearing an army uniform."

"How about I drive, and you man the gun this time, Princess Warrior?"

"Can you drive with a broken ankle?"

"Is your car an automatic or a stick?"

"Automatic." She winked at him.

He laughed as he hobbled over and slid in the driver's seat of her Mustang. "Nice ride, Princess." Jack almost purred at the thought of the horsepower below the hood.

She smiled and tucked her Glock in her waistband, behind her back. She jumped in the backseat and slapped the last magazine in the AR-15, pulled the charging handle, and released the bolt. "Game on, Jack. Better punch it, Jack, the dozer is already halfway there!"

CHAPTER 28

"COLONEL, WORD FROM INSCOM is that your daughter and her colleague are alive and well and requesting a medevac for two injured civilians. They will identify the LZ with green smoke, on the other side of the compound," the captain announced over the radio.

"Thank you, Captain. Dispatch Greenbean10 for the medevac to the McConnell airbase hospital as soon as the firing ceases."

* * *

Diane counted four terrorists positioned on the back end of the bulldozer's engine. She placed the driver in the gun sights of her AR-15 and squeezed four rounds toward the cab. There was no response from the driver.

"I'm positive I hit him, Jack."

The terrorists returned fire. Jack sped up as a hail of gunfire kicked up dust all around and behind them. Diane returned fire, hitting one as he rolled off to the ground.

"Hold on, Diane!" Jack hollered, turning the steering wheel sharply toward the front of the bulldozer. Jack pulled just inches in front of the massive blade. He employed the dozer blade as a shield against the terrorists riding on the back end, blocking their shots.

"I know full well I hit my target, Jack. Something is not right. I believe the damn driver is a dummy, I think it has a remote control or something!"

Jack moved the rearview mirror around and used it to look at the dozer. There was a small instrument panel with a short antenna mounted to the roof of the cab.

"Shoot the control panel on the roof of the cab, now!" Jack yelled.

She rose to her knees on the edge of the rear seat, her back resting on the backside of the front passenger seat, and pumped eight bullets into the control box. Sparks flew as it fell to the ground.

"That didn't disable it, Jack. I've got to get on that damn thing to stop it!"

Jack zigzagged the car back and forth so she could take a shot at the terrorists riding on the back. She emptied the ammo in the AR-15 and two more terrorists dropped from the bulldozer. She reached around and took her Glock from her waistband.

"We're running out of time. You have to go now, Diane."

She climbed over the front seat. "You get behind it. I'll jump from the hood." Carefully, she climbed over the windshield and got into position, kneeling on the hood with one hand grasping the top of the windshield and a pistol in her other hand.

Jack slowed and maneuvered behind the bulldozer, hanging over the side and to his left.

A terrorist clung to the handrail with one hand, his opposite hand pointing his AK-47. He wildly unloaded a burst of ammo on full auto. Bullets punched holes down the length of the driver's side of the Mustang. An awful searing pain burned the left side of Jack's jerking body.

Diane returned fire, shooting the terrorist four times point-blank in the chest. She leaped on top of the engine cover, grabbed on to a handrail with her left hand, and pulled herself up.

Jack began to lose feeling on his left side; his fingers and toes went numb. He lifted his foot off the gas pedal, slowed to a halt, and placed the car in park. Jack could feel a warm trickle of blood from his chest run down the inside of his shirt. He went from sheer panic to a calm peaceful state, knowing he was likely going to die. Memories of his kid sister and his dog, Sugar—the last two who genuinely loved him, flooded his thoughts.

He leaned over and rested his head against the door.

A bright reflection peeked in his eyes, sunlight off a radio knob. The shape of an angel appeared to him, then the angel slowly faded into darkness.

"Jack... Jack..." Diane called as she watched him pass out and slump over. "No, Jack, damn it!" Tears filled her eyes. She looked into the cab of the dozer she was still clinging to. There was a plastic mannequin sitting in the seat, with four bullet holes in its torso. She could see Chris's dump truck straight ahead. She searched for keys to turn off the diesel engine, but there weren't any. Fear set in. She had maybe ten seconds to disable the bulldozer.

THE BLACKBIRD THREAT

Standing on top of the engine cover, Diane unlatched and raised it. She frantically began pulling wires and cables connected to the engine. It sputtered as she grasped one last wire and pulled it so hard she slammed the back of her head on the engine cover. The bulldozer rolled to a stop just as it hit Chris's dump truck. She fell backward over the handrail and onto the ground. Bleeding and disoriented, she struggled to her feet. Her thigh was bleeding from contact with the corner of the engine cover.

She staggered toward her Mustang.

Jack, please be alive.

She glanced skyward, hoping to catch sight of an airborne Black Hawk. To her surprise, she saw a Y-shaped tail on the aircraft coming in her direction. She recognized it as an MQ-9 Air Force drone and leaped with joy. "Hi, Max!" she shouted. She made every effort to get the operator's attention by jumping up and down, waving her arms in a wild celebration.

"SNAFU-9er, this is ground control, we have a lock on the target vehicle. Launching on target in three, two, one." A slight puff of smoke appeared under the right wing. An air-to-surface Hellfire missile was launched directly at the bulldozer.

Diane's heart was pounding out of her chest. There was no escaping the missile. She took five long strides and dove to the ground. In one motion she drew her knees to her chest, wrapped her arms around her head, and curled up into a ball. She positioned her back toward the bulldozer, praying the bulletproof vest would offer some protection. She took one last deep breath of air as the Hellfire missile roared past, ten feet above the ground.

The tremendous blast engulfed her in a cloud of dust and threw her several feet in the air. Stabbing pain radiated from the blast pressure, concentrating in her ears, lungs, and stomach. Stunned and disoriented, she lost consciousness.

"SNAFU-9er, this is ground control. Target destroyed. Sector cleared and returning to base."

"Copy that, ground control," replied the captain.

Katia watched through Jack's binoculars. She grabbed her cell phone and searched for recent calls. She called the number she didn't recognize. "Max, I think they might have just killed Diane and Jack. A drone just fired a missile on top of them," she cried. She flung her cell phone and cried out, "They're coming!"

Katia pulled the pin on the green smoke grenade and tossed it in front of the Suburban as a Black Hawk rose above the horizon.

Greenbean10 landed twenty meters from the Suburban, on the top of the mound. Two medics jumped out and attended to Deputy Iverson and Chris. Katia hurried over and informed the pilot, "We have to go down there and pick up Diane and Jack. They are seriously injured, if they are not already dead."

The pilot and copilot quickly helped carry the deputy and Chris into the Black Hawk. They were loaded and airborne within a minute and a half.

"SNAFU-9er, this is Greenbean10. Be advised we picked up the two wounded. Picking up the colonel's daughter and her partner, status unknown, and inbound to McConnell Air Force Base hospital," reported the Greenbean10 pilot.

"Copy that. SNAFU-9er out."

CHAPTER 29

THE COLONEL RAISED his fist and signaled for the squad to halt. He knelt on one knee and looked through his binoculars, scanning the training center grounds. "Captain, why the hell is Greenbean10 landing on the far side of the compound?" he demanded.

"They are picking up the injured agents and performing CPR on one as we speak. Sir, they are reporting that there's a hot nuke in the silo."

The colonel closed his eyes and looked down. "The person receiving the CPR... male or female?"

"Male, sir."

The colonel took a deep breath in and let it out slowly. "Keep me posted on their conditions, captain."

He pressed his mic button. "This is Colonel Glass, we have a situation here... possible code PINNACLE NUCFLASH! We need the NEST ASAP! We believe a missile, armed with a nuclear warhead, is in a hostile silo currently blocked by a dump truck parked on top of it, preventing its launch.

"Most, if not all, the resistance aboveground has been terminated. We are in a stalemate. We have no way to enter the bunker or silo. If hostile forces remain active below ground, there still exists the threat of detonation. The ball is in your court, gentlemen. I await your suggestions."

"Standby, Colonel," General Martin replied.

"Roger that, sir."

Colonel Glass sought out the first sergeant. "Take three men and secure a perimeter around the ranch house, report any movement. Do not engage unless ordered."

* * *

"This is SRT Greenbean10, inbound. Be advised I have three males and one female in critical condition. ETA seven minutes, requesting a trauma team meet us at the LZ."

"Greenbean10, the base is closed and under orders to evacuate, outward bound only. Everyone except first responders. Suggest rerouting to Topeka or Tulsa outside of the evacuation zone."

"Negative, orders are to deliver to McConnell, now! I have direct orders from Colonel Glass, and his orders are coming from the White House. Copy that?"

"Greenbean10, can we have an assessment of their injuries?"

"One has four gunshot wounds along the left side, from his calf to his chest. He's in shock. Victim number two has a gunshot wound to the leg, shattered femur. He's also in shock. Victim number three has a large stab wound, entering near the top of the left scapula, downward to the left lung. Victim four is a twenty-eight-year-old female with head trauma. She is unconscious.

She has some shrapnel wounds on her arms, legs, and bleeding from her ears, nose, and mouth. Vitals are low."

"Greenbean10, we need their names and ranks, so we can pull their medical files."

"Negative, all civilians. Two federal investigators, one deputy sheriff, and a truck driver."

"Copy that, Greenbean10."

"ETA three minutes. Greenbean10 out."

CHAPTER 30

July 3 at 3:53 p.m.
White House Situation Room

THE PRESIDENT'S CHIEF of staff entered the situation room and announced, "The president is returning on Air Force One, arriving in thirty minutes." He pointed to Max. "Max, do we know who is behind this missile crisis?"

"Yes, sir. I really wish I could talk to our people, but Jack is in surgery, and he and Diane are both on life support. Here is what I have pieced together from the investigation so far. We believe a team of terrorists built a multi-stage rocket. We tracked purchases of thirty-two thousand gallons of RP-1 kerosene and six thousand gallons of liquid oxygen, with an additional twenty-four thousand gallons of liquid oxygen from a distributor located in Canada. My Air Force intel sources tell me this is enough fuel for a large rocket, capable of delivering a nuclear payload."

"What was their target?"

"I have no hard evidence of any particular location. Jack, my lead investigator on the ground, believed the rocket was to create a massive EMP explosion that would take out our national power grid and most of Canada and Mexico's as well."

"Gentlemen, do we have any idea how long it would take to evacuate the Wichita area?" asked the chief of staff.

"No one can say with any certainty. There is a population

of approximately six hundred thousand in that part of Kansas. We have a news blackout on this event. I did order all overflights near Wichita to be re-routed or delayed. FEMA is inbound with command and control. Utilities have been notified, local officials notified, and a slow and controlled evacuation is now underway. Kansas State Police are blocking inbound traffic on all interstates. Schools, medical personnel, and then parents are the first to be evacuated. We have a NEST inbound to the silo site. ETA twenty minutes," Max replied.

"NEST?" he asked.

"Nuclear Emergency Response Team, a team made up of scientists, engineers, and technicians, under the Department of Home-land Security.

"Well done, Max"

"Thank you, sir."

"Gentlemen, assuming the worst, here are some points to consider. What will the cover story be? How do we explain a nuclear explosion in Kansas? And if we say it was a terrorist attack... who is to blame? Who do we want to blame? Meaning, never let an emergency go to waste. This is a once-in-a-generation opportunity," said the CIA director.

"Are you suggesting we frame another country, whether they had anything to do with this terrorist threat or not?" asked Max.

"I'm saying America will never stand for talk and debates on who, or why, but rather how we completely destroyed their country in return. It does open the door for a preemptive first strike attack against Iran and/or North Korea."

"Are you willing to take responsibility for Israel being invaded, dragging Russia or China into the conflict, and probably starting World War Three? Because if word gets out that big, badass America nuked small countries away with a first strike, we will be the most hated country in the history of the world," the chief of staff replied.

"You can't sacrifice six hundred thousand Americans in the name of world peace! Someone has to pay! That's just the way it is. No one would know. We can and will produce all the evidence we need for the UN or anyone else in the world who doubts us," said the CIA director.

Max shook his head in disgust and stepped out into the hallway to escape the madness. Leaning back against the wall, he took off his necktie and dabbed the sweat off his forehead.

"Are you okay, sir?" asked a White House staffer as he walked down the hall.

"I'm fine," he replied. He called his wife and it went straight to voicemail. "Hey, this is going to be an extra long night. I want you to pack some supplies for our safe room. Keep the kids close by… just in case. Developments are not looking very good at the moment. Some unacceptable conditions are about to happen. Love you, and I'll talk to you later."

"Max, please step back into the room. We have a new intel report coming in from the NSA," General Martin called.

The chief of staff passed out copies of the report. "Take a minute and dissect this. Max, can you give us your take on this intel?"

"The first set of numbers is rocket fuel transactions, banks, and routing numbers. As you can see, the payments came from a bank in Yemen. The second set of transactions is from an offshore bank in the Bahamas, routing numbers to a shell company in Topeka, and into the professor's bank account."

"Why didn't this raise any red flags?"

"I don't know.

"The next set of numbers is wire transfers from a Swiss bank account to the offshore Bahamas bank. The next set of wire transfers is from a Swiss bank account to the bank in Yemen.

"Following the money trail leads us back to this Swiss bank account, owned by an international investment firm controlled by Victor Borso, multi-billionaire globalist. Victor's hobby is to cause chaos and harm to non-European Union nations," Max concluded.

"Max, do you know how ridiculous you sound? Half of our government is made up of globalist. You're really reaching with Victor!" said the CIA director.

"I know you have ties with Borso. And you, sir, are not without suspicion!" shouted Max.

The chief of staff held up his hand. "Gentle-men, this type of discourse will not help the situation in Wichita!"

"I say we reach out to Borso and offer twenty billion in gold, and immunity, if he surrenders the nuke to our NEST personell. What do we have to lose? It could buy us some valuable time," Max pleaded.

CHAPTER 31

THE AIR FORCE C-130 transport looked even bigger with just a handful of men sitting near the end of the cargo fuselage. The constant sound of the four turboprop engines gave four of the five NEST members a sick feeling–but for one, the sound was that of an old friend.

Bill Cragg, a nuclear scientist and electrical engineer, gave the jumpmaster a handshake. "I can't believe I'm doing a HALO jump again. I thought my final tour as a SEAL would be the last jump from thirty thousand feet. Hell, that was over twenty years ago."

"Don't worry, it's just like riding a bike. Every time you fall down, it hurts like hell," laughed the jumpmaster.

Bill was a natural leader, and being a former Special Ops member made him an ideal NEST team leader. He turned and looked at his team. Each of them looked scared to death.

"Guys, I know this is not what you signed up for, but this is the only way to get us to the target area. Okay, check your oxygen mask, then take several deep breaths." He checked his watch. "We have been on oxygen for twenty-eight minutes so far. You have to purge the nitrogen from your bloodstream or you could get the bends.

"All of you will be jumping in tandem with a Special Ops operator. Do what he says, because he is your lifeline.

"Outside the aircraft, it's something like forty degrees below zero. Be ready for a big chill. Don't worry, though, 'cause it's ninety-something degrees on the ground.

"You will freefall for up to two minutes, so don't be frightened. It's a planned freefall.

"Once we are on the ground, move south toward the smoke screen. Our guys on the ground will meet us there. Do you copy?"

His five team members nodded, still looking scared to death. Just what you would expect from folks who had never parachuted before.

"Check your harness connections with your partner. You have three minutes to the drop zone," the jumpmaster announced.

The large cargo door at the back of the plane slowly lowered and turned into the off-ramp. There was a sudden roar of the engines and the sound of air drag against the descending ramp door. The chill of the air rushed into the plane. The jumpmaster hooked a parachute, attached to a crate, to the static line. He pushed the crate, containing tools and equipment, out the back of the plane.

"Line up on the back edge of the ramp. Ready? Go! Go! Go!"

One after another the men ran and jumped off the ramp, two seconds apart. Bill, being the last to jump, yelled at the jumpmaster, "Thanks, chief," and gave him a thumbs-up as he dove off the ramp.

CHAPTER 32

"COLONEL, THE C-130 is here and the HALO jump is now in progress," reported the captain.

"Take six men and set off smoke grenades in a straight line, ten meters apart. It'll give them some cover. Then escort them back here." Glass surveyed the old maintenance building. "This will be our command post as of now."

"Yes, sir."

"Colonel, what is our game plan?" asked the second lieutenant, concerned.

The colonel looked the lieutenant in the eyes as he put his hand on his shoulder. "Son, we have to get these NEST team members inside the bunker to disarm this nuke."

The colonel saw a hopeless look in the eyes of the lieutenant. "Look, it's not over until you see a big flash. Until then, we have our work cut out for us. Lieutenant, take as many men as you need. I want a set of eyes on all escape hatches, air vents, or anything protruding from the ground. Report any movement, but do not engage unless ordered."

"Yes, sir, right away."

CHAPTER 33

TWO SECRET SERVICE agents entered the room. One of the agents said in a loud voice, "Gentlemen, the President of the United States."

The other agent walked to the front and stood in the corner of the room.

The president entered the Situation Room. "How in the hell did we get here, gentlemen? What are our best options for handling this attack?"

Everyone looked at Max.

"Mr. President, I'm not sure how up-to-date you are with this crisis."

Max's assistant, Annie, entered the room. "Sorry to interrupt, gentlemen, I think this is important." She handed Max a report.

"Thank you, Annie."

She smiled, nodded, and quickly left the room.

"I have heard every word on the way here. We have no time to be politically correct right now. I agree with the CIA that somebody has to pay, and pay a heavy price," replied the pre-sident.

"This report I just received confirmed my point about Victor Boros. He dumped seven hundred and fifty million shares in American oil and gas stocks three weeks ago. He immediately purchased British Petroleum and various Russian natural gas stocks." Max kept scanning the papers Annie handed him. "Victor also recently invested five billion dollars in an international shipping company, Aqua Freightliner Express LTD., and a hundred million in a Singapore electronics supplier. Don't you see his plan?" Max asked in a pleading tone. "A terrorist attack on America takes down the national power grid. Tens of millions die from violence over evaporating food and water supplies. American production comes to a screeching halt. The stock market crashes. World markets panic, causing oil prices to soar. And then the world's largest rescue mission gets underway to save the dying superpower. Thousands of ships and aircraft deliver food, medicine, and supplies." Max took a deep breath and plunged on. "Victor makes fifty billion dollars on his investments, while making the European Union the new superpower. Global elites seize the financial power for the final piece of the new one-world government system. Meanwhile, America's military annihilates Iran, and/or North Korea, which is being blamed for the terrorist attack. All nicely set up by Victor hiring Islamic terrorists to do all his dirty work." Max put the report down in front of the president. "Thanks to my field agents, we don't have to face the EMP threat. Victor's masterplan has failed. The only leverage he has on us is the nuke. So, Mr. President, you know Victor Boros personally. And we know he is responsible for financing the terrorist plot. So my question is this: Can he be bought off if he knows that we know he is responsible and that we will kill him if this nuke detonates? Do you think, with him being a businessman, that being paid a ten-to-twenty-billion-dollar ransom in gold, and immunity from prosecution, would be enough for him to abort this terrorist threat?

"As many as six hundred thousand Americans could live or die based on your answer, Mr. President!"

CHAPTER 34

"COLONEL, MY NAME is Bill Cragg. I'm the NEST team leader. We deployed here as fast as we could. I brought four other members with me. What do we have?"

"Gather 'round, men." The colonel motioned for everyone to stand around an old, rusty steel workbench with the colonel's open laptop on it. He pointed his finger at his laptop. "Displayed on my laptop is an aerial picture of this missile training center from 1964. You can see from the photo that there were two separate missile silos. Each silo has its own launch control room, a classroom, and a section where the living quarters are located, one level below the launch room.

"This photo, taken last year, shows a two-story house built over the entrance to launch control room number one. Silo two has the original old missile sliding doors. Silo one has a newer type of missile door that intel suggests is based on a smaller Russian hatch design.

"See this long depression in the ground? Intel believes a tunnel was recently constructed connecting the two silo systems. The silo walls are three-foot thick reinforced cement. The tunnels and the launch control rooms are twenty to thirty feet underground. Air shafts are too small for a human to fit into. Each silo has a single escape hatch that closes and locks from the inside only. The main entrance door is steel fourteen inches thick." The colonel pointed at his laptop screen. "We are standing here, in this garage or maintenance building.

There is also a radar or radio building over on the far side of silo number two."

"Colonel, how do you propose we get my men inside the bunker?" asked Bill.

"I was hoping maybe you had a sugges-tion."

"We haven't figured that one out yet," replied the colonel.

"Well, in the meantime, I can transmit a jamming signal. However, when I begin transmitting, you won't be able to send a signal out, and all communications will be cut off. You might want to notify central command we're going silent."

The colonel turned to the captain. "Send the message."

"Yes, sir."

"Bill, your team can set up your gear here in this maintenance building. It looks like we are about fifty meters away from silo one. What are the chances the rocket can be fired with remote radio controls?" asked the colonel.

"Thankfully, not on a rocket of this size, Colonel. The jamming signal is to overload any radio signals and prevent detonating the warhead. That doesn't mean we are out of the woods yet. There may be other controls that could trigger the warhead as well. The liftoff control systems are always hardwired and controlled inside the silo structure on liquid propelled rockets of this size."

The lieutenant turned to Glass. "Colonel, we are seeing movement around the escape hatch of silo one."

"Don't let that hatch door close! We are on our way," ordered the colonel. "Let's go, Bill, this may be our only chance."

Bill snatched up his tool bag as the colonel picked up his M4 assault rifle. NEST team members Travis Goen and James Lytle grabbed their gear and followed. Once outside, they were joined by the two remaining NEST members and the three Special Ops soldiers assigned to protect them.

Five terrorists climbed out of the escape hatch, which was no larger than a standard manhole cover. Three of them were armed with AK-47 assault rifles, and the other two each had rocket-propelled grenades. They slowly crawled into a prone position and spread out, two meters apart, facing silo one. The leader shouted commands in Arabic. Both rocket-propelled grenades hit Chris's dump truck simultaneously. There was a tremendous explosion of fire as the fuel tank exploded. It sent flames a hundred feet into the sky and lifted the heavy truck a foot above the silo hatch door. Stone and metal fragments filled the air, along with a rising column of thick black smoke from the melting tires.

Chris's dump truck still remained partially on the silo door despite taking two direct hits. The silo door repeatedly rose and lowered only a few more inches.

The colonel hand-signaled his team to rush the escape hatch. Muzzle flashes flew from the terrorists' AK-47s, now pointed directly at them. They fired back while advancing toward the escape hatch. Two of the terrorists reloaded their RPG launchers and readied themselves to fire again on the dump truck.

One yelled at the other in Arabic, "Three, two, one, fire!" Another direct hit on the dump truck nearly pushed it off the hatch. Now the door rose up to at a thirty-degree angle.

Tracer bullets whizzed through the air as dust clouds from the ground exploded all around the Special Ops members running in a mad dash to get to the escape hatch.

Two of the terrorists fell. Two Special Ops soldiers and two NEST members all hit the ground, either killed or wounded. The colonel fired his weapon in full auto, desperate to stop the terrorists as they started to descend back into the thirty-foot deep escape tunnel.

The last remaining terrorist emptied his AK-47. He attempted to reload, only a few feet in front of the escape hatch door, when a bullet struck his right thigh. He screamed and staggered backward two steps, falling to the ground. He tried to crawl toward the open hatch door.

The colonel, Bill, James Lytle, and Travis Goen closed in on the escape hatch as the injured terrorist was starting down the metal stairs.

"Grab the hatch door, Bill!" shouted the colonel as he took two steps and lunged for the terrorist, latching onto his arm just above the wrist.

The terrorist wildly swung his other clenched fist at the colonel's face.

Bill reached over the top of the escape door and jerked it open past ninety degrees just as a burst from an AK-47 fired from below, missing Bill's face by inches.

Travis Goen caught and grabbed the terrorist's other arm.

He screamed in Arabic, "Do not let the infidels take me!"

A burst from an AK-47 riddled the terrorist from the chest down. They pulled his limp, bloody body out of the escape hatch opening.

The colonel turned to Bill and his team. "Gentlemen, we have to go down there. Grab your gear and follow me." He spotted the lieutenant checking vitals on a downed NEST member twenty meters away. He shouted to the lieutenant, "Get six men and follow us down inside the escape hatch!"

"Yes, sir."

Colonel Glass removed a tactical flashlight from his pocket and attached it to his M4 assault rifle. He removed his sidearm from his holster and handed the pistol to Bill. "Cover me on the way down." He slung his rifle over his shoulder, with the barrel pointing down, lighting his way below as he began his descent on the steep metal stairs. "Watch your step. They're covered with blood. Slippery as hell."

"James, grab that dead guy's AK-47 and magazine. I'll take them." Bill held out his hand.

The colonel was at the bottom of the stairs, looking around at a small oval-shaped corridor connected to the main tunnel. The tunnel was thirty degrees cooler than the surface, but under the circumstances, it felt more like death in the musty, cool, dark hole. Colonel Glass nearly lost his balance on the empty shell casings littering the floor. He kicked them out of the way.

"Clear," he called. "Bill, you and your team can come on down."

James handed Bill the AK-47 and Bill gave James the colonel's pistol. Bill slung the rifle and his backpack over his shoulder and headed down the stairs. James and Travis picked up their backpacks and equipment to follow.

The lieutenant and five more Special Ops soldiers arrived just as Travis started down the steps of the ladder. "Sergeant, stay topside and guard the opening and the captain will guard the silo. Report any changes," ordered the lieutenant.

"Yes, sir."

"Bill, how do you suggest we disarm this damn thing?" asked the colonel when Bill made it down to him.

"If you cut off the head, the body dies."

"I agree. So where do we start?"

The two were standing at an opening connected to to the main tunnel, which was made out of round galvanized ribbed steel sections twelve feet in diameter, welded together, with a poured cement floor. After nearly sixty years of neglect, surface rust covered most of the walls, and a history of groundwater leaks gave the tunnel a sickening, musty smell.

"If we turn right, it should take us to the control room, and a left turn should take us to the silo." The colonel shined his rifle-mounted flashlight at the ceiling light fixture in the pitch-black tunnel. "Shutting the lights off definitely feels like an ambush. There must be more of them down here.

"Lieutenant, we'll toss grenades down each tunnel and lay down automatic fire in both directions. You take your men to the control room. If you get past the blast doors that protect it, blow it to hell. You are my rearguard, and your mission is to prevent any terrorists from leaving the control room. The sergeant and I will escort the NEST team to the silo."

"Yes, sir."

The soldiers lined up near the opening to the tunnel. Two of the soldiers pulled the pins on their grenades and tossed them toward opposite ends of the tunnel. The explosions, less than a second apart, rocked the tunnel and filled the air with smoke. Shots rang out from the direction of the control room. The soldiers returned fire, emptying and reloading their weapons twice.

Believing it to be safe after a moment of complete silence, the lieutenant and his men entered in attack mode. Each soldier was wearing night vision goggles, and their M4-A1 assault weapons were equipped with green lasers. Moving slowly, one after another, and alternating left and right sides of the tunnel, the laser lights looked like small lighthouse beams sweeping over a dark ocean.

The lieutenant carefully maneuvered his men around and over four dead terrorists. He raised his hand and signaled his men to stop. He heard one of his soldiers stumble. A large explosion rocked the tunnel, killing three of the Special Ops soldiers instantly. The blast threw the lieutenant face-first into the tunnel wall.

With ringing ears and disoriented by the blinding light, he sat in total darkness. He touched his face, ears, and nose to make sure every part was still there. A burning pain sped from his right foot to his knee. He felt from his knee down and realized most of his foot was gone. He could only assume one of the soldiers accidentally triggered an IED.

"Lieutenant, are you hurt?"

"Is that you, Shadow?"

"Yes, sir. I can't feel my left arm, but other than that I'm okay," reported Master Sergeant Shadow Hawk.

He was a warrior in the truest sense–a twelve year Army Ranger and veteran of three tours in Iraq, a weapons specialist, and an expert in hand-to-hand combat. He'd been awarded one Silver Star, two Bronze Stars, and two Purple Hearts.

"Shadow, give me a hand. I've got a bad wheel, and I lost my night vision. What is the status of the team?"

The sergeant looked over the area through his night goggles. "All killed, sir. It's just you and me."

Unimaginable sorrow overcame him. His whole team gone. They were going to pay for this.

He pulled off his belt and started to tie off his ankle above the missing foot. "Help me find my damn goggles."

After locating the goggles, the two soldiers piled up seven dead bodies in front of them, building a wall of flesh for cover. They placed their dead friends' weapons next to them so they didn't have to stop to reload. They lay in each other's blood and waited.

CHAPTER 35

"COLONEL, THAT DIDN'T sound like a grenade to me," the sergeant said.

"You're right. It sounded much stronger. Watch it, eyes at eleven o'clock. There is the tunnel going to the other silo," cautioned the colonel. "Sergeant, go scope it out to see if it's clear of any tangos."

Bill made sure the AK-47 was locked and loaded, then he started walking behind the sergeant.

"Whoa, Bill… I'll cover him. I know you're an ex-SEAL, but we are here to guard you, not the other way around."

"Sorry, Colonel. For a second, my instincts got the better of me."

The colonel nodded in understanding. "Once a warrior, always a warrior."

The sergeant stood next to the tunnel opening to the other silo. He took a deep breath and peeked around the corner. "Clear as far as I can see, Colonel."

Colonel Glass had a bad feeling about passing in front of the twelve-foot-wide ope-ning. He motioned Bill to bring his team to him. "Okay, men, after the sergeant makes it across, Bill, you and your team go one at a time. I'll cover you and then the sergeant can cover me. You copy?"

"Yes, sir," they replied in unison.

Colonel Glass placed his gun sights just inside the dark tunnel, taking aim at the center space. "Ready whenever you are, Sergeant."

Bill gave the sergeant a good-luck pat on the back.

The sergeant ran in a crouched position across the opening without shots fired.

Bill then sent Travis over, followed by James.

The colonel looked over at Bill. "If I don't make it, the silo should be the next opening."

"Roger that, Colonel, but you're going too. We can't finish this mission without you." He saluted the colonel, then dashed across.

Just as the colonel began to cross, a white light blinded him and he stumbled back. The lights in the tunnel were suddenly back on. He flipped his night vision goggles up and out of the way as automatic fire began at the other end of the silo two tunnel. He motioned to Bill to run to the silo as explosions went off near the control room and all hell broke loose.

The sergeant fired a long burst as a dozen or so tangos ran toward them from the other, adjoining silo complex.

The colonel took a few steps, then dove into a forward roll. He sprung up to his feet in one motion while firing his weapon in full auto. The tangos were in a prone position, firing back with an RPG. The rocket hit the tunnel wall, sending metal fragments everywhere. The explosion propelled the colonel back several feet, where he landed face-down. He got back up and pulled the pin on a hand grenade. He tossed it in the direction of the terrorists. He waited a few seconds, then he tossed another one. After a few seconds of silence, he heard automatic fire coming from the control room, where his men were still engaging the terrorists.

Kneeling over the sergeant, he checked his vitals–all strong. "Come on, my friend, you're going with me." He took one last look inside the connecting tunnel to silo two, then fired a burst inside the tunnel. There was no return fire. He picked up the sergeant, threw him over his shoulder, and headed to silo one.

Bill and James were leaning over a handrail on a metal landing overlooking the rocket.

"Damn, that's a huge warhead. Maybe the largest I've ever seen. The rest is old-school. See the elevator? It has to raise the rocket to the surface before it can be fired. There are no exhaust shafts," pointed out Bill.

Twenty feet above them, the hatch suddenly slammed closed, but quickly began opening again, the loud sound echoing throughout the silo. Each time, Chris's dump truck slid farther and farther off the top of the hatch door, the door opening wider.

Travis, standing in the middle of the silo doorway, spotted the colonel coming toward him through the dust and smoke, carrying the sergeant over his shoulder. He ran to assist him. They each grabbed one of the sergeant's arms and wrapped them around their necks to drag him. The slumped sergeant's toes scraped tracks on the floor.

"Captain, are you still up there?" shouted Colonel Glass as he looked up at the top of the silo.

"Yes, sir, Colonel."

"Send the rest of the men down the escape hatch, and reinforce the men near the control room. On the double, Captain!"

"Yes, sir, Colonel."

The colonel and captain both realized if this rocket blew up, or the nuke detonated, all would be vaporized, but at least with his men underground, they had a slim fighting chance to survive.

Travis and James were a few steps behind the colonel as

they descended the forty-foot steel ladder to the silo floor.

Bill leaned over the handrail and pointed to an access panel just above the thrust chambers. "This one here, Travis. Check and see if there are any valves or switches inside the panel. I'm looking for a way to override or shut down the fuel and liquid oxygen pumps."

The colonel was standing guard in the doorway, listening to the automatic gunfire coming from near the control room. His thoughts suddenly switched to Diane. He imagined her lying in a hospital bed on life support. He blamed himself for her condition, because he was the one that pulled strings so she would be chosen for this assignment. His world was starting to unravel.

The mechanical groans from the silo hatch door suddenly stopped. Daylight poured in from the top of the unobstructed silo opening. Suddenly a loud horn blasted three short intervals.

Bill shouted to Travis and James, "Hurry, we only have seconds now! That was the warning alarm to clear the area!"

Bill watched Travis and James jump off the ladder, dropping the last ten feet to the floor.

Travis reached his hand down to assist James up to his feet. A hot pain exploded in his ribcage and his head slammed into the floor. He felt the weight of his attacker on top of him. He threw his hands up as he saw a knife plunging toward his neck.

James grabbed the pistol he was carrying and aimed for the attacker.

"Don't shoot! You could blow up the damn silo!" screamed Bill.

James dropped the gun and rushed to pull the attacker off

Travis. Another terrorist charged him from the far side of the rocket and stabbed him in the upper chest. Both fell to the ground and wrestled for control of the knife.

Travis managed to stop the knife just as the blade entered the left side of his throat. He felt blood running to the nape of his neck. Only his adrenalin surge was giving him the strength to keep fighting off his assailant.

Seeing his men stabbed and fighting for their lives, Bill jumped on the ladder. No time to use the ladder rungs–he placed his boots and hands on the outsides of the vertical pipe ladder. Using his boots as brakes, he did a controlled fall four stories down to the bottom of the ladder, burning and ripping the skin off his fingers in the process.

After descending to the bottom, Bill sensed Travis was losing his fight with the terrorist on top of him. He lunged behind the terrorist, but as he grabbed him the man turned and drove the knife into Bill's hip socket, cutting the muscles and tendons. He stumbled but managed to hold on to him, snapping the man's neck before they both fell to the ground.

The loud hum of an electric motor as it began running was quickly followed by a noise from large hydraulic pumps. The elevator began to slowly lift the massive rocket platform to the liftoff position above the surface.

Bill finally subdued the terrorist and dropped the bloody knife. Unable to stand, he watched as the rocket escaped his grasp.

James finally overcame his attacker. Bloody and battered, barely able to move, they sat, horrified, knowing that once the rocket engines ignited they would be cremated alive.

The colonel shouted to Bill, "What the hell is happening? What can I do to help?"

"The umbilical cords, disconnect the umbilical cords."

"Where are they?" He was leaning over the guardrail, trying to hear their reply.

Bill and James pointed straight up in the air.

"Climb up the gantry, Colonel!" shouted Bill.

To the colonel, the gantry looked like a giant TV antenna, like the one his father had on his farmhouse back in the 1950s. It was made up of 4 fifty-foot poles connected by metal straps four feet apart, forming a tall rectangular tower. A four-inch steel conduit placed in the center contained the three umbilical cords. The base was reinforced and bolted to the rocket platform. Two hydraulic cylinders, attached to a giant hinge in their bases, allowed the gantry tower to unclamp the rocket and tilt away from it at liftoff. A mixture of old and new technology.

The colonel laid his weapon down, climbed over the guardrail and onto the pipe ladder. He stretched out as far as his six-foot-two frame would allow but kept one hand and one foot on the ladder. He was still well short of reaching the moving gantry. He looked down at the NEST team as they watched him. He placed both hands behind him on the ladder, with both feet facing the gantry.

"Is he doing what I think he is he doing?" asked James, anxiously.

"Yeah. If he misses, we are all dead."

They held their breath and watched helplessly.

Okay... okay... I have to time this exactly right... God help me.

He bent his knees, pushed off, and half-screamed, half-growled. He stretched out like a flying squirrel. His momentum carried him wide, left of the gantry, and he missed the crossbar. He desperately grasped at the outside pole of the gantry. The sudden stop jerked his body sideways and he fell back, slamming hard into the rail and banging his face against the metal, breaking his nose. He grasped with his left hand and wrapped his legs around the pole. He wiped at his bleeding nose with his shirtsleeve and shimmed upward to the crossbar. He threw his right leg over the rod and pulled himself up and onto his feet. He reached over and tugged violently on the lowest and smallest umbilical cord. As soon as it detached, he shimmed farther up the pole to the next crossbar and pulled himself up to the next section.

"Yes, yes, Colonel! You're getting it, but hurry, man!" shouted Bill as he pumped his fist in the air.

The rocket and gantry were rising to the surface at a rate of one foot every two seconds. Now twenty feet above the ground and rising, the colonel reached the second umbilical cord, which was twice the circumference of the first one. Unable to shake it loose, he climbed above the cable, then stepped down, keeping one hand on the crossbar. He began to jump up and down with both feet until it detached from the rocket. He nearly fell at one point but managed to catch a foothold on a crossbar and reclaim his balance. The rocket was now thirty-five feet above the surface and still rising. The colonel looked down at the NEST team, nine stories below him.

Damn, that was a close one.

The heat was beginning to take its toll on his body. Inside the underground silo the temperature was a constant sixty degrees, but outside the summer day exceeded ninety degrees. He wiped the sweat from his forehead to keep it from burning his eyes. He leaned back his head a moment to try and get his nose to stop bleeding.

Come on, damn it, only six more feet.

He finally reached the last umbilical cord, at the top of the gantry. It ran through a six-foot metal arm and dropped over to the rocket. The colonel was startled by the gantry's sudden tilt away from the rocket. He grasped the structure tightly, holding on until the arm dropped and locked into place.

Straddling the arm between his legs, he slid down and tried to move the umbilical cord. He took a deep, steadying breath and, even with all his might, he failed to budge the arm.

His only recourse was to slide out on the arm and yank the cable in hopes it would disconnect from the damn rocket.

The arm was made of a four-inch square tubular steel section. The colonel, drenched in sweat, leaned over and very slowly stretched out with his on each side of the arm while squeezing it with his knees and ankles.

Shit, this is nuts! It's like climbing out on a flagpole on a five-story building. What I wouldn't give for a Black Hawk and a long rope ladder.

Fighting to maintain his balance, the colonel placed both hands on the umbilical cord. He pulled but nothing happened. He tried swinging the cord left to right, but it remained connected. The rocket started to emit a high whining sound.

Shit! The damn thing is going to lift off with me out here!

"What is the colonel thinking?" James screamed over the noise of the rocket ramping up to launch.

"He can't disconnect the last cable. Say a prayer for us, James. We are about to meet our maker."

James started reciting the twenty-third Psalm.

The colonel pulled himself out onto the one-and-a-half-inch thick cable, hand-over-hand, eight to ten inches at a time until his feet slid off the arm. Losing his balance, he slid down the cable, yet managed to cling to the cable with only his sweaty right hand. Dangling and desperately fighting to keep his hold, he grimaced as he swung sideways until he caught the cable with his left hand. He was now hanging five stories from the bottom of the platform, swinging wildly.

He grasped a new hold each time his legs swung toward the missile until he got close enough to catch his feet on the side of the rocket.

Pulling back on the cable with his arms and pushing off the side of the rocket with his feet, he managed to maneuver close enough to see the connector. He quickly realized the cable automatically disconnected after the rocket engine ignited. There was a recessed handle above the connector and the words 'manual release' painted in red.

Thank you, Jesus!

He stretched his fingers but could not quite reach the handle. There was a deafening sound coming from the base of the rocket, letting him know he was almost out of time. In desperation, he lunged for the handle as the rocket engine attempted to ignite. When his fingertips caught the handle, the cable disconnected, sending him tumbling down headfirst. He screamed as pain shot through his shoulder, but he managed to hang on. He was dangling at the end of the cable as it swung back in the direction of the gantry.

Bill looked at James as he leaned over, pumped his fist in the air, and shouted, "He did it. The son of a bitch did it!"

"Lieutenant, look, there's someone hanging off the missile tower."

"I'm going down to take a look, get ready to toss down a

rope."

"Yes, sir," replied the crew chief.

The colonel watched as the Black Hawk passed in front of the sun, making a wide arc in the sky as it came toward him. Tears filled his eyes and ran down his face, mixing with the blood from his broken nose.

Hurry, boys, I can't hold on forever.

The crew chief stood at the open side door, looking down at the missile and the man hanging on to a cable.

"Holy shit! That's the colonel, Lieutenant!" shouted the crew chief.

"Quick, get that rope out, Chief," shouted the pilot.

The lieutenant of Greenbean10 quickly and skillfully maneuvered the rope to the colonel.

Grabbing the life-line with his left hand and wrapping it around his leg, he gave the crew chief a thumbs-up.

The chief quickly reeled the colonel up and inside the Black Hawk.

The colonel smiled up at them as they leaned over him on the floor of the helicopter. "Man, am I glad to see you guys."

They exchanged pats on the back as the colonel made it to his feet.

He was still trying to regain his balance as he staggered up between the pilots. "Okay, the missile is disabled. I have three wounded NEST team members at the bottom of the silo. A dozen or more of my team are inside the tunnel leading to the control room. We need reinforcements, now!"

"Look, Colonel." The pilot pointed through the cockpit window.

Slowly circling the old training center, six Black Hawks

began to land, two near the ranch house, two at the open escape hatch, and two near the silo. The Special Ops soldiers raced out of the Black Hawks and entered each location.

"Colonel, permission to pick up the wounded and medevac to the McConnell Air Force Base hospital? Oh, and I took the liberty of asking the trauma specialist about your daughter. She is responding to the treatment well and he said she is expected to recover. Do you copy, Colonel?"

The colonel had the greatest burden lifted from his shoulders. He smiled at the pilot in relief. "Roger that, Lieutenant. Roger that."

CHAPTER 36

One Year Later...

A SHINY BLACK stretch limousine arrived in front of the Trump International Hotel's lobby entrance.

"The limo is here! Isn't this exciting, Chris?" Katia asked.

"This whole thing really hasn't sunk in yet."

"Your wife isn't coming?" Katia asked.

"Marcee and my daughter, Julie, are flying in with Cindy and her daughter, Jenny. She will meet us there."

"Here, let me help you," Katia offered.

"No, no, I'm good. I need the practice on this new leg. It's a balance and timing thing."

The doorman held the door for them as they walked out to stand underneath the canopy. The door on the limo opened and out stepped a tall man in a dark blue suit, white shirt, and a bright red necktie.

A big grin appeared on Katia's face, her eyes smiling at the man. "Hi, Ron, I almost didn't recognize you. You're out of uniform, Deputy," she joked as she gave him a hug.

"I was instructed not to wear my uniform because the events that happened are still classified and my sleeves give away the name and location of my department," Ron replied.

"Oh, God, it will be interesting to see how they expect to pull this whole thing off," she said.

"Hey, Deputy," Chris called.

"How's the leg? Better?" Ron asked.

"Just getting acquainted with it. I got it in the mail the other day. It's the new and improved one, with the greatest rating and lowest price, according to Amazon. Four and three-quarter stars! Got one hell of a deal and, of course, free shipping."

They all laughed at his joke.

With the help of Ron and Katia, Chris entered the limo first. Inside sat a man with a dark complexion and dark hair, wearing a black suit with a blue tie.

Chris smiled and offered the man his hand. "Hi, my name is Chris Finley."

"I'm Master Sergeant Shadow Hawk, Special Ops."

"So you were there?"

"Yes, with one of Colonel Glass's teams."

Chris gripped his hand firmly. "Well, welcome to the party."

"Katia, have you ever ridden in a limo before?" Ron asked.

"No, never. This is such a surreal experience for me."

Ron opened a bottle of Krug champagne. Katia held two champagne glasses in each hand and Ron took them from her one at a time, filling them with champagne. He handed them out. "A toast! God bless America and God bless each of us."

They each said, "Cheers," and tapped their glasses together.

It was a special treat to ride together in the limo to the White House. Each one realized how amazing it was to have survived the terrorist attack. The experience they'd had together would be everlasting.

By the time they finished their toast, the limo had pulled up to the White House's guard station at the gate. After checking IDs and the guest list, the guard instructed the driver to take them to the Rose Garden.

"Follow me, please." A White House aide–a short blonde lady in her early twenties–kept looking between her smartphone in one hand and a large tablet in the other. She walked faster and mumbled, "Oh, damn it."

"I'm guessing this is her first rodeo," Ron joked.

The aide looked at Ron. "Nope, second one. These things never go as planned, and I've only been here since April.

"Okay, Chris, you will sit in the second chair in the front row, going right to left behind this side of the podium. Katia, you will sit beside Chris in chair three, Ron in chair four. Chairs five, six, and seven are for the NEST team. Has anybody seen the NEST team?" she asked. "Sergeant Hawk, you are sitting in the second seat in row two. You'll be sitting next to Colonel Glass. Got it?"

"Yes, ma'am," he replied.

She answered her cell. "Okay, okay, I was worried they would miss the ceremony… And the military personnel? Well, tell them to hurry the hell up! I need them in their seats in five minutes!"

Katia waved at the White House aide. "Can you tell me who is sitting in this first chair? Is it Diane Glass?"

Looking very annoyed, she said, "Just a minute." The aide waved at a member of the press. "You can't take pictures or video from there! You must stand in the roped-in area directly behind these chairs. And any faces, other than the ones in the front row, facing you, must be blurred. Failure to do so will cost you your passes for future events. Understood? Good!" She turned back toward Katia. "Max Braude is sitting there."

Katia wondered, *Where are they going to seat Diane*?

As the seats quickly began to fill in the guest section, a man with a salt and pepper beard wearing aviator sunglasses, a grey suit, white shirt, and a teal necktie walked down the aisle, making his way slowly to the front row. He saw a pretty woman with bright red lipstick and long dark brown hair. She was wearing a black dinner dress, black stilettos, and a tan basketweave hat with a large black bow and white roses circling the wide brim.

"Excuse me, is this seat taken?" he asked.

"No, not unless the chair Nazi makes you move."

"Chair Nazi?"

"The lady with the cell phone and tablet in her hand. Whatever you do, don't make eye contact. Keep your glasses on, Jack."

"Aww, I thought I had you fooled, Diane."

"I had you ID'd before I laid eyes on you, the second I smelled your cologne.

"Jack, on my left is my supervisor, Karen Waters."

"Nice to me you, Karen. I want to thank you for all your support. Without those satellite pictures, Diane and I might not be here today!"

"You're very welcome, Jack. What you and Diane did was miraculous."

"I think we both had angels on our shoul-ders," he replied.

Diane caught Katia's eye up on the stage and gave her a thumbs-up.

Katia threw her hands out, palms up. "Why are you not up here? And what's with the hair?"

Diane put her index finger up to her lips as she shook her head *no*.

"I'm happy to see Max get some recog-nition, at last. He's the best!" Jack said.

"I agree, he really did a fine job." Diane nodded.

The press secretary strolled up to the microphone. "Ladies and gentlemen, the Presi-dent of the United States." The president shook hands with the press secretary, and the secre-tary sat down.

Chris waved at his wife and daughter, sitting in the first row on the other side of the aisle from Jack and Diane.

His wife waved back and blew him a kiss.

Ron waved at his family, seated in the first and second rows behind Chris's family.

"Thank you, thank you. What a beautiful morning it is here in the Rose Garden. Before we get started with the ceremony, I have an announcement to make. As you know, there has been a considerable amount of friction between myself and the Director of the CIA. Therefore, as of today, Max Braude will be the new Director of the CIA. We are ready to move forward, working together to repair the lost trust of many Americans. And we are ready to tackle the many security issues facing America and our allies.

"Now, we are here today to pay honor to some fallen heroes who died defending our wonderful country.

"Two worked for the FBI, seven were soldiers in Special Operations, and two were federal employees. I cannot share any details on how they died. This is an ongoing federal investigation into a terrorist attack. I can tell you this–it was huge, very huge! Once the investigation is declassified, I'm sure books will be written and movies will be made. But for now, folks, that is all I'm allowed to say. We are officially declaring that a terrorist attack occurred–we must do this for certain benefits to apply to our military families. These brave individuals made the ultimate sacrifice, and as a grateful country we honor them.

"I have several medals to award today in a closed-to-the-public ceremony in the beautiful Rose Garden. When the gag order is lifted and the events come to light, you are going to be very, very proud of these folks. Just as I am now.

"Thank you. Now I must ask the news media to leave. We must protect the identities of some of our intelligence operatives here on the grounds today. Thank you, thank you very much."

Pandemonium broke out among the repor-ters.

"Mr. President! Mr. President!" they shou-ted.

"Mr. President, did the former CIA director resign or was he fired?"

"I will tell you this... the result is the same," replied the president. "Thank you. Now you must go," he insisted.

White House aides and a few Secret Service personnel began assisting the news media's exit from the Rose Garden.

The president, with Colonel Glass assisting, began awarding Purple Heart medals to the families of the fallen soldiers.

Katia wiped the tears from her eyes as a wife and three small children received the Purple Heart medal from the president.

He placed it on the shirt of the oldest son. "America will always be grateful to your father, and we honor him today." The president shook the young boy's hand.

"Sergeant Shadow Hawk, a true warrior in every sense of the word. His great-great-grandfather was the great Sioux chief, Sitting Bull. Sergeant Hawk was wounded by an IED and his team was reduced to just himself and his badly wounded and dying lieutenant.

"He single-handedly fought and killed eighteen terrorists in a fierce firefight, allowing the NEST team and Colonel

Glass to disarm the nuclear missile. For your actions and bravery, I am proud to award you the Congressional Medal Of Honor." The president hung the medal around the sergeant's neck and shook his hand.

The sergeant received a very long and loud round of applause.

"Congratulations, Sergeant."

"Thank you, Mr. President."

They exchanged handshakes and saluted each other. Sergeant Hawk was straight-faced while receiving his medal.

Diane saw a tear in the corner of the sergeant's eye. She could tell he was suffering from PTSD. She had seen that look on many of her dad's team who returned from Iraq. She quickly looked away.

I wonder if I'm not suffering from PTSD too?

Next came the medals for the NEST team. First, the president gave awards to the families of the two fallen team members. Then he presented the DOE Medal of Valor to Travis Goen, James Lytle, and Bill Cragg.

"These brave men jumped out of a C130 at thirty thousand feet. Four of the five had never parachuted before. They ran toward bullets aimed at them, fought hand-to-hand with terrorists, and prevented the loss of life of hundreds of thousands of Americans." The president applauded them.

The audience went wild with cheers and applause for the surviving NEST members.

"Chris Finley, it is my honor to award you the Medal of Freedom. This is the nation's highest honor given to a non-government person. You risked it all and gave much to your country. Our nation is grateful." The president shook his hand and patted him on the back.

"Katia Rochet, it is my honor to award you the National

Intelligence Medal of Valor. America thanks you for your actions and great courage."

She shook the president's hand and gave him a quick hug.

"Deputy Ron Iverson, it is my honor to award you the Medal of Valor, which is the highest honor given to a law enforcement officer."

"Thank you, Mr. President." Ron flashed a big smile and exchanged a firm handshake with the president.

The White House aide, crouching down low, walked up to Diane and Jack. "You're up next!"

Diane looked at Jack and rolled her eyes.

Jack smiled at the aide. Jack stood and held his hand out to Diane. "Come on, Princess Warrior."

She smiled and took his hand.

They stepped up on stage. They took a moment to shake hands with Ron, Katia, Chris, and Max as they walked past them to stand behind the president.

"Before I award the last two medals, I have a story to tell. My son saw these medals sitting on my desk in the Oval Office. He asked me, 'Dad, which is worth more, one of these medals or a Super Bowl ring?'

"I said, 'Son, if it wasn't for these medals, there would never ever be another Super Bowl.' He replied, 'Oh, cool.'"

The small audience roared with laughter.

"So, there you have it. I'm very happy to award the National Intelligence Cross Medal to Michael 'Jack' Jacobs. I was told your heart stopped beating three times from your gunshot wounds."

"Yes sir, Mr. President. I've never been much of a quitter. My goal is to one day drain my federal pension plan," Jack joked.

"I hope you can stick around and help me send those

terrorists back to where they belong?" the president said.

Jack smiled, shook the president's hand, and took a step back. "Step up here, Diane."

"Diane Glass. Her dad nicknamed her Princess Warrior. She is the daughter of Special Forces Commander Colonel Jim Glass. That's right, the same Colonel Glass standing beside me. And I suspect he will be promoted to Brigadier General soon." He turned and shook the colonel's hand. "When I read the report on what happened, I said, 'Oh, my God, she really is a princess warrior!'

"Diane Glass, I am proud to award you the National Intelligence Cross medal."

"Thank you, Mr. President. I'm honored to be of service to our wonderful country!"

"America sure is proud of you. Once word gets out, you may want to hire an agent. Endorsements will be pouring in, I'm sure."

She shook the president's hand and stepped back.

"Diane, Katia, and Chris, wait here. I need to a have word with you.

"Okay, folks, this concludes the medal ceremony. Enjoy the brunch, and there will be White House tours available afterward. Thank you."

Jack noticed Max standing nearby.

"Congrats, Max. This is kind of a shock, I didn't see this coming."

"It's a bit of a shock for me too. How is your recovery going? Back to normal?"

"Still going to physical therapy, but at least I can walk now."

"I don't need an answer today, but I want you to consider

coming back to the agency. I need someone I can trust, someone who has my back. I know the reason you left. I promise you, I will have your back. What do you say, Jack, still want to save the world?"

Diane grabbed Chris's medal, hanging from the ribbon around his neck, and rubbed the Medal of Freedom with her thumb. "This is very cool, and I'm so happy you received it." She gave Chris a hug and turned to hug Katia.

Chris's wife and her friend Cindy approached the stage.

"Diane and Katia, have you met my wife, Marcee, and our good friend, Cindy?"

"Hi, Marcee. I'm Diane."

"I wanted to take this opportunity to thank you for saving my husband's life." Marcee gave Diane a long tight hug.

"You're welcome, but Chris and Katia saved us as well." Diane looked at Cindy. "Do you remember me? I promised you dinner if we made it. Would a brunch at the White House do?"

They all laughed at Diane's joke.

"You look so much better than I remember. You really clean up well. I love your hat, those white roses are really beautiful. But I thought you were a blonde?" Cindy commented.

"I am a blonde. I'm sort of undercover at the moment. Where are your daughters, ladies?"

"One of the first lady's personal aides took the girls on a special private tour of the White House. Kitchens, bathrooms, and closets. And other places visitors are forbidden to see," Marcee added.

"The girls were so excited, really beaming," Cindy exclaimed.

The president, three Secret Service agents, Max, and Jack all strolled up.

The president began by shaking hands with Marcee and Cindy. "I can't tell you how proud I am of all you folks. Diane, I understand your Mustang got destroyed. I was telling my good friend, Jerry, who is the vice president of Ford Motor Company's high-performance division, about what happened to you and your car. And he said, 'I have a solution to her problem.' Jerry started a foundation for American heroes, where corporations can make donations and recognize individuals who, through their courage, help America or Americans." The president reached into his left jacket pocket and pulled out a key fob with a key ring tag that read 'Princess Warrior.' "Diane, this is yours. It is a brand-new test vehicle." He began to read off a three-by-five file card. "An Oxford White Shelby GT350 five-hundred and twenty-six horsepower Mustang convertible with a black interior."

"Mr. President, I don't know what to say. Thank you very, very much."

"I'll have my secretary send you Jerry's phone and mailing address. You can thank him. Oh, I almost forgot. Katia, I was told how jealous you were of Diane's car." He reached into his right pocket and pulled out a key fob with a key ring marked 'Katmobile.'

"Here is your new Katmobile. It's the same as Diane's, except it's in Shadow Black, with a black interior."

Surprised, Katia's jaw dropped and she just stared at the president. "I'm speechless, Mr. Pre-sident."

The president smiled. "I really have the best friends, Katia."

He turned to Chris. "I understand you mortgaged your

home to buy the dump truck for your business, and the insurance would not cover the damage done by the terrorists. Which is typical, I guess. I was told there was a GoFundMe account in your name. Enough money was raised to put food on the table and help make payments on your truck because you were unable to work. Is that right?"

"Yes, sir, Mr. President. I have wonderful friends too," Chris replied.

"More than you know, Chris, more than you know. With the influx of wounded warriors returning from the Middle East, the Veterans Administration has been working closely with a company called Handicap Theologies of Indiana. The results have been amazing, giving vets newfound freedom of movement. My friends at Caterpillar have a special vehicle. They have donated to you a brand-new tri-axel dump truck.

"Now, as I have been told, you had your left leg amputated high above the knee, and you can never drive a truck with a clutch again. This truck has electronic paddle shift pedals, located on the steering wheel, and is the first of its kind in the nation." The president reached inside his breast coat pocket, pulled out an envelope, and handed it to Chris. "Here is the title to your old truck, and also your house mortgage is paid in full. My personal gift to you. As long as I am president, we will never leave a soldier on the battlefield, or leave them when they return home. Chris, you're very welcome from a grateful country.

"Oh, I almost forgot, you have been added to the preferred vendor list for all federal construction work in Kansas and the surrounding states. I predict you will soon have a fleet of dump trucks and drivers," the president added.

Marcee could no longer contain her emotions and began to jump up and down, with tears streaming down her face.

"Oh, my God... Oh, my God... Permission to hug you, Mr. President?"

The president smiled. "Permission gran-ted."

Hugs and handshakes broke out at that moment of celebration. Each of the Secret Service agents took the time to shake Chris's hand. There were few dry eyes in the group.

A tap on his back startled Jack and he quickly turned.

"Hi, Jack, remember me?" asked a serious- looking Linell, from the procurement office. "You said you would take good care of my vehicle and my equipment. It was a total loss and cost my department three hundred and seventy-three thousand dollars. Well, what the hell, Jack? What were you possibly thinking? I wouldn't notice?" she asked in a huff.

"I'm—I'm very sorry, Linell. I would pay you back, but I would need a serious pay raise," he stammered in return.

"Oh hell, Jack, I'm just messing with you. It was worth every damn penny!" She laughed and gave him a hug. "Just don't do it again. You hear?"

CHAPTER 37

Three Weeks Later...
8:41 a.m.
Brussels, Belgium

A **WINDOW ON** the fourth story opened quietly and a steady summer breeze rushed in on the warm, sunny morning. The aroma of coffee from the apartment next door seeped through the window.

She stuck her head out the window, looking down on the dozen or so small tables with red and white umbrellas, shielding the hungry customers from the sun, at the cafe downstairs. Across the narrow street, in front of the old brick building, was a four-city-block-square park. Magnolia trees, located in the center of the park, divided the playground equipment from the rest of the park, and a duck pond, surrounded by trees, offered shade to a couple sitting on one of the park benches.

She set an old black guitar case on the dining room table and slid the table across the old oak floor, stopping eight feet behind the open window. She flipped open the latches on the guitar case and pulled back tightly on her black leather gloves, making sure she felt her fingertips in the ends of both gloves.

Glancing down at her watch, she quickly removed the upper receiver of the fifty-caliber Russian sniper rifle from the case, attached the lower receiver, and flipped down the bipod.

Next, she attached the telescoping sights and installed a large sound suppressor to the barrel. She drew back the bolt and inserted a five-and-a-half-inch long cartridge, slid the bolt forward, and locked it into place. She calmly walked over to an old hi-fi stereo turntable and selected an old vinyl record from the stack. She chose an old seventies rock album. Lifting the arm, she gently set the needle on the record, turned the volume control past halfway, and quickly lit three scented candles.

She observed the couple on the park bench. She adjusted the crosshairs and drew a bead on the man's right temple. Slowly she moved over to the woman's face.

Behind the woman and across the street was a Euro Finance and Investment Center, which had gold-tinted mirrored glass windows on each of its nine stories. It was one of many twenty-first century buildings in the forward-thinking capital of Belgium–home to NATO and one of the cities competing to be the new capital of Europe. The finance center sat on the corner across from the park, with a one-way street on the east side of the building. The other side of the street was a large brick department store.

From her vantage point, she could view three blocks down the one-way street to a traffic light. She glanced at her watch, waiting for his limousine to arrive promptly at 9:00 a.m.

Three minutes later, a new black Mercedes Maybach S600 armored limousine stopped at the red light. She tracked the limo in her scope until it pulled over to the curb, parking in a loading zone.

She calculated the distance, factoring in that she was firing into the wind, and a descending forty-foot bullet drop.

First out of the limo was Bodyguard Number One, exiting

the front passenger side door. He scanned the sidewalk and anyone close to the limo. The second bodyguard exited the passenger door on the driver's side. He scanned the department store beside them, across the street. The third bodyguard slid out of the rear passenger side door and stepped to the back of the limo.

The target slid out of the limo and stood between the two bodyguards.

She placed the crosshairs on the center of the first bodyguard's forehead. He took two steps in her direction. She squeezed the trigger. Her body jerked back from the recoil of the powerful rifle. The bullet missed the first bodyguard's head by inches and hit her target center mass, exploding his heart and spinal cord. He was dead before his body dropped to the sidewalk. The path of the bullet also struck the bodyguard standing behind the target, shattering his pelvis. Unable to stand, he fell to the sidewalk.

The bodyguard in front ducked in behind the limo door and called 1-1-2, the European equivalent of 9-1-1, on his cell phone.

The bodyguard on the driver's side of the limo dragged the injured bodyguard to safety behind the car.

She ejected the hot, spent cartridge, stood the casing up on the table, *this is for Doug and Joe* and wrote Воин принцессы (Princess Warrior in Russian) with red lipstick, and left a white rose on the table. She grabbed her backpack and removed two smoke grenades. Quickly she slipped the backpack on, then locked the apartment door behind her and walked down the hall to the elevator. The door opened on the empty elevator. She pressed floors three, two, and one, then pulled the pins on the smoke grenades and tossed them in the elevator as the doors closed.

She pulled the fire alarm switch beside the elevator and ran down the stairs shouting, *"Feuer... Feuer,"* in German and *"Feu... Feu,"* in French.

Pandemonium broke out in the apartment building as smoke poured onto each floor. She reached the ground floor and ran out the rear exit door. A red BMW 750 GS motorcycle awaited just a few steps away. She climbed on and sped away, blending into the heavy traffic as the fire trucks and ambulances arrived.

Sitting and waiting for a traffic light to change, she made a call on her cell phone. "Victor Bravo is down. I repeat, Victor Bravo is down."

The End of the Blackbird Threat.

CASE CLOSED

ABOUT THE AUTHOR

Growing up in Indiana during the fifties and sixties, I enjoyed reading comic books and watching black-and-white TV on the only three channels available. One of my favorite shows was the Lone Ranger. He and Tonto never failed to save the town or a beautiful girl, only to leave town and on to their next adventure. This simple plot and storyline must have worked well because it appears in every action series with a variation of this simple script. Later on, shows with mystery and suspense like Alfred Hitchcock, Mission Impossible, and Twilight Zone would peak my young imagination and a desire to write was born.

Fast forward fifty plus years after a long intermission, also known as a thing called life, with my three children grown. Now retired with a slight case of empty nest syndrome, the desire to write returned with a vengeance. With the ideas and plots connected, dipped in current events and a tad of tongue-in-cheek storyline, I wrote my first book <u>The Blackbird Threat.</u>